Havana Confidential

David Pereda

AmErica House
Baltimore

First printing

ISBN: 1-59129-244-1
PUBLISHED BY AMERICA HOUSE BOOK PUBLISHERS
www.publishamerica.com
Baltimore

Printed in the United States of America

For

Elinor and Luis

For my
Friends Alfonso &
Marina Campagnas—
My First Published Novel
Read it !

[signature]

Miami
4/10/03

PS — The story is about
Finished Arconza

ACKNOWLEDGEMENTS

I gratefully acknowledge the help, and the patience, of Dr. Graham Tercero-Graham in explaining to me the correct medical procedure during a heart attack; as well as his revision of that portion of my manuscript. I recognize also the assistance of Doctors Elizabeth de Legorreta and Marian Lon Blanco in matters pertaining to plastic surgery and general medicine, respectively.

My special recognition and heartfelt thanks go to Lizbeth Nucamendi, who supervised the manuscript preparation and coordinated every minute detail that went into putting the entire package together.

To my agent, Karen Carr, and my editors, my deepest gratitude…

BOOK ONE

CHAPTER I

Raymond wondered if, after thirty years, he would recognize his childhood friend Pepe. With growing excitement, he watched the bustling front door of the crowded Cuban restaurant in Miami's "Little Havana" where they had agreed to meet for lunch. Pepe's hoarse voice conveyed an urgent message when, unexpectedly, he telephoned Raymond's medical office in Palm Beach two days earlier.

"*Hola*, Ramón!" a gravelly voice said next to him. "*Qué gusto verte*! How *are* you, Doctor Peters?"

Raymond bolted with surprise and stared, speechless, at the big man dressed in faded jeans and a white polo that had materialized out of nowhere and was now standing by his table. The features had been ravaged and distorted by age, and the mop of dark hair had been replaced by a balding grizzly gray, but he recognized immediately the man who once was his best friend growing up in Cuba.

"Pepe Orozco," Raymond said. "You haven't changed."

Pepe broke out with laughter, making his face appear boyish despite all the wrinkles – and suddenly sharp and disconnected memories flooded Raymond's mind as he remembered when they were both kids attending catholic school in Havana. Pepe's childish grin hadn't changed.

"Hell, don't lie to me, Ramón. I'm forty pounds heavier than when we played baseball in Cuba." He paused, turning serious. "I'm glad you could come down to Miami on a busy Friday to have lunch with me."

"I'm on vacation. The summer months are slow for me, so I usually take the entire month of August off." Raymond gave a vague shrug and added, "Besides, I was curious. After all, I hadn't heard from you in thirty years – and it sounded urgent."

"It *is* urgent." Pepe sat across from Raymond. "Believe me."

9

"Well, here I am. I'm all ears."

"Yes, here you are – the famous Doctor Peters."

"You're not being ironical, I hope. I heard from you last during the Bay of Pigs invasion, and I still came all the way down to Miami to meet you. If you're being ironical–"

"I'm not being ironical," Pepe interrupted him, smiling disarmingly. "I'm grateful you came – really. It was just a comment."

Raymond scrutinized Pepe's face, trying to ascertain whether his friend was being flippant or not. He couldn't.

"I thought you were dead," he finally said.

"Obviously I'm not."

"Where have you been all this time, Pepe?" Raymond asked. "Tell me."

"Around."

"Around?"

"Nicaragua, Watergate, Afghanistan, Angola and a couple of other places I'd rather forget."

"The military?"

"The CIA."

"How come you never–" Raymond started angrily, but was silenced by a forceful motion from Pepe.

"*Porque no pude*, Ramón," Pepe said abruptly. "I couldn't. It was better for you I didn't contact you. Besides, you weren't very interested anyway."

"What do you mean?"

"You weren't very interested in anything Cuban, Ramón. You became a world-known plastic surgeon, changed your Spanish name to Raymond Peters, and became a famous multi-millionaire living in a posh area of Palm Beach – with friends like Pitanguy, DeBakey and Anthony Quinn."

"It was better for my career to have an Anglo name then."

"Why, Ramón? Were you afraid of being discriminated against?"

"Yes, I was, Pepe. There was a lot of discrimination against Cubans thirty years ago. Now it doesn't matter. Things are different now, more open."

"I never changed my name to an Anglo name."

"Maybe you were never considered as director of a medical school in Texas either, or were you?"

"You know I wasn't."

"What do you want from me, Pepe? Surely you didn't call me here, after all this time, to criticize me for changing my name."

"No."

"Why did you call me then?"

"Because you need me."

"*I* need you?"

"That's right. You have a problem, and I want to help you solve it."

"You have a lot of cheek, Pepe. You, my best friend, disappear from my life for thirty years, just like that, and reappear again to tell me I have a problem? *No jodas.* Screw you! You're nuts!"

Raymond got to his feet angrily, rattling the table. Several diners stared at him.

"Sit down, Ramón!" Pepe commanded. "I didn't want to call you; I *had* to call you, you understand? And if I left you alone all these years, it was for your own good, *comprendes*?"

Raymond sat down slowly. He took a deep breath, trying to relax. He hadn't been so furious in years.

"That's better," Pepe said. "Why don't we order something to eat? I'm hungry, aren't you?"

He waved the waiter over. The restaurant was filling up with the usual lunch crowd – Cuban businessmen, American tourists from up north looking for excitement and a taste of *frijoles negros*, and refined old ladies seeking nostalgia.

"What do you want from me, Pepe?" Raymond asked.

"I want you to go to Cuba with me."

"Why should I go to Cuba with you, Pepe? I haven't wanted to go to Cuba since I came to the States. Besides, I don't even know if I can go. I'm an American citizen, and I don't know if the U.S. government would let me go."

"You can go, don't worry about that," Pepe said. "I'll arrange it for you literally hassle-free. Leave that to me."

"Why should I go, Pepe? I have no family in Cuba anymore. My only uncle died a few years back."

"To see your son."

"*My* son? What son, Pepe?" Raymond thought he hadn't heard

11

well. "I have no son. My wife died less than a year ago in an automobile accident. To my eternal regret, we had no children."

"I recommend the *carne asada*," a voice said. "The roast beef - and also, the yellow-rice and chicken. Very good too."

"What?" Raymond was dazed. "You what?"

As in a fog, he realized it was the waiter. Dressed in a white short-sleeve shirt with black pants and bow tie, the young man smiled at him. He couldn't have been older than eighteen.

"*Carne asada*," Pepe ordered. "With black beans and rice and green plantains."

"Me too," Raymond said.

The waiter took the order and left.

"Remember Sonia?" Pepe asked.

"Of course I remember Sonia. I've often wondered what became of her."

"She stayed in Cuba working for the revolution, got married, and had a son."

"That's nice, I guess."

"*Your* son."

"I beg your pardon?"

"Sonia had your son."

The waiter returned with steaming platters of white rice, fried plantains, black beans and *carne asada*. He set them on the table, a broad smile on his face.

"*Buen provecho*," he said, and left.

Raymond's heart pounded. A paralyzing chill gripped his stomach. He wasn't hungry anymore.

"What did you say, Pepe?"

"Sonia was pregnant when you left Cuba. You were so intent on leaving, she didn't have the heart to tell you anything." Pepe gave him a curious look. "Are you feeling okay? You don't look so good."

"I'm fine," Raymond lied. "Since when have you known all this?"

"Since the beginning."

"Why didn't you tell me anything?"

"Sonia didn't want me to." Pepe served himself a heaping plate, which reminded Raymond of how much he used to eat when they were kids. "So I never told you."

"You've been in touch with her all these years?"

Pepe nodded, his mouth full.

"Why tell me now? What has changed now?"

"Eat," Pepe said. "The *carne asada* is good, and the *frijoles* are excellent. You don't get this good Cuban cooking in Palm Beach, or do you? You ought to eat something."

"I'm not hungry." Raymond felt nauseous. "How old is my son?"

"Thirty-two."

"What does he do?"

"He's a doctor like you." Pepe laughed, gulping down his food rapidly "A cardiologist specialist in sports medicine. Funny, isn't it? Your son is a doctor too. Must be genetic."

"What's different now, Pepe? My son hasn't wanted to see me in thirty-two years, and neither has his mother, so why the sudden change?"

"He's very ill."

Pepe put his knife and fork down and leaned back. He stared at Raymond with appraising eyes. The din of the diners had increased to a shrill cacophony, but Raymond's attention was riveted on his friend.

"Ill?"

"Cancer," Pepe said. "Lymphatic cancer. He has less than twelve months to live, and he wants to meet his father. You can understand that, can't you?"

Raymond let his breath out explosively. His mouth was dry, and the nauseous feeling in his stomach was making him dizzy. Reaching forward, he grabbed his glass of water with both hands and sipped from it. His hands trembled. The cold liquid helped relax him.

"Yes." He nodded.

"Yes what?"

"Yes, I can understand that."

"That means you'll do it?"

Raymond thought a moment, his mind a jumble of contradictory ideas and potential actions. He took a deep breath and let it out slowly.

"I don't think so, Pepe." We're total strangers. It might be better if I let him die in peace. I don't even know what he looks like."

Pepe pulled out a color snapshot from his wallet and handed it to him.

"Here's a recent picture of him." Pepe gave him a sad smile. "He sent it to you."

Raymond stared at a young man with a smiling face dressed in a white doctor's smock. On the back there was an inscription written in black ink on a tight scrawl: *Para Ramón, de Mon.*

"Mon?" Raymond asked. "His name is Ramón too?"

"Sonia named him after you." Pepe took the picture from his friend's hands and studied it. "He looks a lot like you."

Raymond nodded, overwhelmed. He had noticed the resemblance.

"Do you have a picture of Sonia too?" he asked.

"No."

"Have you seen her lately?"

"Yes."

"What does she look like?"

"As pretty as ever, thirty years later."

"How could we go to Cuba, Pepe? Ask for permission from the American government?"

"Leave that to me."

"I want to know."

"We'll go via Mexico. The Mexican government will give us fake passports."

"The Mexican government is in on it too?"

Pepe nodded.

"Is there something you're not telling me, Pepe?"

Pepe stopped chewing. He stared at Raymond deadpan, his head cocked, not a muscle moving on his face. Raymond thought he detected a hint of a smile on his lips.

"There *is* something, isn't there, Pepe?"

Pepe shrugged, non-committal, saying nothing.

"And you're coming with me to Cuba?"

Pepe nodded, chewing again.

"Why?"

"It's safer for you that way. Both your son and Sonia are members of the Cuban resistance. Anything goes wrong while you're there, and you could be in a lot of trouble."

"Isn't it dangerous for you?"

"Sure." Pepe shrugged. "Crossing the street is dangerous too.

Depends on how you do it."

Raymond leaned back in his chair. The restaurant was full. His stomach felt cold and hard as a frozen instant dinner.

"How are things in Cuba nowadays?"

"Ask Ramiro. He just came from there. He arrived in a raft with all his family – his wife and two kids."

"Who's Ramiro?"

"The waiter. The young man who has been serving us food."

"You know him?"

"I do. I helped him get out of Cuba." Pepe looked behind Raymond and made a motion with his hand. "Ramiro, *ven acá un momento*! Come here, please."

The young man hurried over, a smile on his face.

"*Sí, Señor* Orozco?"

"Tell Doctor Peters how things are in Cuba. He wants to know."

"You don't really want to know how things are in Cuba, Doctor Peters. You'll be depressed."

"Try me."

"*Las cosas están muy malas, muy malas*." Ramiro made a face. "Things are very bad in Cuba. Forget about riding on Chinese bikes, everybody knows about that." Ramiro's hands were a blur of constant motion as he explained. "There's television only two hours a day, except Saturdays when it's four hours, mostly propaganda. You need a penicillin injection, you must go to a hospital – drugstores are closed. At six o'clock everyday the electricity is cut. Women use boiled rags for Tampax and bathe with herbs – there is no soap. There is no toothpaste either. People brush their teeth with carbon. You want me to go on, Doctor Peters?"

"My God," Raymond said. "Living conditions are awful."

"There's no food," Ramiro went on. "People cut the skin of a grapefruit, which is thick, bread it and fry it, and pretend they eat steak."

"It's depressing."

"Since the government has no money to buy chicken feed, now they give people newborn chicks so they can grow them at home and eat them." Ramiro was no longer smiling. "I lost my oldest daughter in Cuba for lack of food and medicine. That's why I smile all the time now – because I'm happy to be here, in the United States. You want me to go on, Doctor Peters?"

"I believe that's enough, Ramiro," Pepe said softly. "Go take care of another table. Doctor Peters gets the picture."

"My God, Pepe," Raymond said after Ramiro was gone. "Sonia and Ramón live like that?"

Pepe nodded. "Tough, uh?"

"Yes," Raymond replied. "Very tough."

"Well, what do you say, Ramón? Are you coming to Cuba with me or not?"

"Pepe, you're lucky I came down to Miami to meet you." Raymond's voice couldn't conceal his irritation. "I started a month's vacation yesterday. Otherwise, I wouldn't have been able to come. I have a large practice and a responsibility to my patients."

"I appreciate your coming, Ramón. I already told you. Inasmuch as you're on vacation, anyway, why not come down to Cuba with me for a few days?"

"Pepe, if you think I'm going to Cuba with you, you're crazy! *Estás loco.* They kill people in Cuba. How do I know this whole thing isn't a scheme to drag me to Cuba and kill me too?"

"It isn't."

"Who says so?"

"I do."

"Don't make me laugh, Pepe," Raymond said gruffly. "You show up in my life thirty years later and, just like that, ask me to go to Cuba. Why should I believe you? How do I know you're who you say you are? You could be a Castro agent. You could be involved in drugs or something sordid. What do I know?"

"You always had this wild imagination, Ramón." Pepe leaned back and laughed good-humoredly. "I see you haven't changed. I haven't changed either. Remember me?"

"I remember you fine," Raymond answered. "But I have news for you. I've changed a lot over the years – and so have you. I just don't know how yet."

"Indeed I have, Ramón, but not my inner core, my basic personality. That's what I'm referring to. I'm the same, and so are you."

"Don't count on it," Raymond said flatly.

16

Pepe looked at him solemnly. Nodding, he made a noise with his lips like frying eggs.

"Maybe you've *really* changed," he said. "You used to have a high need for adventure when we were kids, a strong sense of loyalty too, and last, but not least, you always paid your debts."

"I still do."

"Then pay *me*."

"I beg your pardon?"

"You owe me one. Pay me."

"What do I owe you?"

"I saved your life when we were kids, remember? We went swimming in that river on a bet from Hermes – remember Hermes?"

"Of course," Raymond replied. "Skinny Hermes with the pimply face."

"That's him. Remember what happened that day?"

"I got caught in a whirlpool and went under. You dove in to save me and almost drowned yourself."

"But I didn't – and neither did you. We got out of it alive together."

Raymond remembered clearly. He nodded.

"So you could say, technically, that all you've done in your life since that day you owe to me," Pepe said. "Isn't that right?"

Raymond nodded absentmindedly, his mind a movie screen playing old films of when he was a kid growing up in Cuba. Until less than an hour ago, Havana seemed like a long time ago. Now he wasn't so sure.

"I'd like you to come to Cuba with me, Ramón," Pepe said. "*Please.* I promised your son. And you owe me one."

"How do I know nothing is going to happen to me in Cuba?"

"I give you my word."

Raymond started to say something, thought better of it and shut up.

"Besides, you're on vacation anyway," Pepe continued. "Take it in Cuba. Aren't you curious to know what Havana looks like today? Don't you want to see Sonia again? What about your son? You were always so inquisitive. You're not anymore?"

Raymond looked at his friend, saying nothing. His mouth felt dry.

"What were you going to do on your vacation?" Pepe asked. "Did you have anything planned?"

"Not really," Raymond answered. "I was planning to spend some time with my mother. She lives on Miami Beach. But mostly I was going to relax, read all the books I didn't read last year, and work on my suntan."

"Is your father still alive?"

"No," Raymond answered. "He died two years ago."

"I'm sorry. What about your brother? Rosendo, right? What happened to him?"

"Roberto," Raymond corrected Pepe. "He's doing quite well. He's an executive for an oil company in Houston. He's married to a nice Texas girl and has three lovely kids, neither of which speaks Spanish – believe it or not."

"Boys or girls?"

"Two girls aged twelve and fifteen, and a boy – nine years old."

"What about you, Ramón?"

"I thought you knew everything about me, Pepe."

"Not all. I know your wife died a year or two ago. You don't have a girlfriend?"

"You sure ask a lot of questions, Pepe."

"I'm curious, Ramón. I haven't seen you in thirty years. You don't have to answer if you don't want to."

"I date a couple of girls." Raymond exhaled loudly.

"Nothing serious?"

"Nothing serious. So far, I haven't found anyone capable of replacing Rebbie."

"Rebbie?"

"My wife. That's how I used to call her. Rebbie – short for Rebecca."

"I see."

"Do you, Pepe?"

"She must have been quite a woman, Ramón."

"She was." Raymond had a lump in his throat. "Rebbie was a self-made woman. She grew up in an orphanage. Her parents died in an automobile accident too, same as she did. Isn't life ironic, Pepe?"

"It sure is, Ramón." Pepe nodded. "It sure is."

"Death is so capricious, Pepe. I've given a lot of thought to death during the past year. Criminals, murderers and drug-pushers die in bed of old age. And Rebbie? A fine surgeon and productive member of society, what happens to her? She dies in a car crash in the prime of her life."

Peep nodded solemnly. "She was a doctor too then?"

"A plastic surgeon like me. We met in medical school. The first time I saw her, she reminded me of a young Sophia Loren. I couldn't believe anyone so beautiful could make such good grades." Raymond sighed then rapped the table, rattling the dishes. "Enough of this! I hate self-pity. If I decided to go, when would we leave?"

"When *could* you leave?"

"I'd have to spend a couple of days with my mother, at least. She's always complaining I never spend anytime with her. But after that—" Raymond's voice trailed off.

"Why don't you spend the weekend with your mother? We could leave on Monday, if that's okay with you."

"Monday is fine."

Pepe nodded, staring at his friend fixedly. He smiled, a boyish grin that brought more childhood memories rushing to Raymond's mind.

"I've always respected you, Ramón," he said. "I want you to know that. You're one of the most ethical people I've ever known. After years surrounded by the dregs of humanity, it restores my faith in mankind to know you're still the same."

"And you've always been an emotional bastard!" Raymond exclaimed. "Let's cut this shit out! You're going to make me cry."

Impulsively, Raymond dipped three fingers in his glass of water and splashed it on his face. He remembered doing the same thing when they were teenagers in Cuba. "See my tears?" he asked.

Pepe roared with laughter, attracting the attention of the diners. "Doctor Peters, you're still the same crazy and unpredictable guy I knew."

"Amen, brother," Raymond said. "I resemble that remark."

"You won't regret it, Ramón," Pepe said softly. "You'll see. *Gracias.*"

"Pepe, *gracias* to you." Raymond grinned at his friend. "I have no wife and no family. For twenty years all my adventures have been confined to the surgery room. I'm *ready* to do something wild. And this is as wild as it gets. Havana, here I come!"

CHAPTER II

Viewed from above, the shape of the brown pollution cloud hovering over the city reminded Raymond of an atomic bomb explosion. When the jetliner dove into the dense mass, heading toward the runway to land, the brown disappeared. Raymond wondered where it all went. He hoped it was not his lungs.

"Mexico City," Pepe said. "The most polluted city in the world – and probably the most congested too."

"I believe it." Raymond observed the heavy traffic flow below. "It's only nine in the morning, and it seems pretty congested already."

"Twenty million people compete for the right to live and breathe all that contamination we saw from the air." Pepe laughed. "That's civilization."

"That's unhealthy," Raymond said.

The plane landed hard, straightened and rolled noisily to a stop at the gate. It was not exactly a great landing, and Raymond wondered if a rookie was piloting the plane. Patiently, the two men waited for clearance to be given by the ground authorities and the door to open. They deplaned, with their carryon bags, onto the gray crowded corridors of Benito Juarez airport.

Two burly men in black suits and Ray Ban sunglasses waited for them by the immigration counters. The taller one held up a sign with their last names on it. Neither man smiled.

"We're Peters and Orozco," Pepe told them.

"Come this way, please, *Señores*," the smaller man said.

Pepe and Raymond followed the two men through customs, without stopping, and onto a black limousine parked outside the exit gate by the curb. The taller man took their bags and tossed them in the trunk of the car.

The smaller man opened the back door of the limousine. Raymond noticed he had cauliflower ears, like a boxer's.

"Inside, please, *Señores*," he said.

Pepe and Raymond did as they were told. The taller man sat in the driver's seat, and the smaller man sat alongside him. Quickly and efficiently, the taller man started the engine and drove off into the heavily transited airport avenue.

"Where is *Licenciado* Ortega?" Pepe asked.

"At the *Secretaria*," the smaller man answered.

"Is it far?"

"*Veinte minutos.*"

They rode in silence through a traffic-congested asphalt maze of city streets until they stopped in front of a large, gray government building.

"*Ya llegamos*," the smaller man announced. "We have arrived."

He got out of the car and opened the door for them. He pointed to the building.

"Go in. The *Licenciado* is expecting you. Second door on the right."

"What about the bags in the trunk?" Pepe asked.

"We'll keep them," he answered. "Pablo and I will be here waiting to take you to your hotel when you finish."

"What's your name?"

"Pedro, *Señor*, at your service." He smiled for the first time, displaying crooked teeth and a gold molar. "Don't worry, *Señor*. We'll wait for you."

Pepe and Raymond marched up the stairs, sidestepping street vendors and beggars. Pepe stopped at the top of the stairs in front of the building, wheezing. He looked pale.

"Wait a moment," he told Raymond. "Please."

"What is it, Pepe?" Raymond asked, concerned. "Are you okay?"

"*Estoy bien*," Pepe replied. "I'm a little short of breath, that's all. It's the altitude. Always takes me a day or two to get my body acclimated to Mexico City."

Raymond watched his friend's color slowly return to normal. Pepe took a deep breath.

"Let's go in," he said. "I'm all right now." Inside, it was dark and musty-smelling. Crowds of people scurried vigorously through the gray linoleum corridors, clutching papers and looking important.

"A typical government office building," Pepe commented. "Everyone runs around looking busy without anything to do."

The second door on the right had a glass panel and a sign above it, which read: *Pasaportes Mexicanos*. Pepe opened it, and they went in.

A single secretary sat behind a graphite-gray metal desk, manicuring her nails in ruby-red. She had big, round gold earrings and a large, red mouth.

"*El Licenciado Ortega, por favor*," Pepe said.

She raised her head to look at him. Her eyes were black.

"He's busy," she said.

"Tell him *Señor* Orozco and *Doctor* Peters are here."

"*Doctor* what?"

"Peters."

She nodded, a hint of interest showing on her face. She appraised her nails first and then Raymond.

"Do you have an appointment with the *Licenciado*?" she asked Raymond.

"*Sí*," Pepe said. "He's expecting us. We just arrived from Miami."

"Ah, the *gringos*," she said. "Why didn't you say so? Go in." She pointed to a closed, gray door behind her. "The *Licenciado* is expecting you."

Licenciado Ortega was chubby, with a big salt-and-pepper moustache and thick gold-rimmed glasses. He stood behind the imposing desk and greeted them cordially. A thin, frizzy-haired man with a flowered tie and no coat stood alongside him.

"This is *Señor* Robles, my assistant," Ortega introduced the other man. "He'll take care of you promptly and have you on your way to Cuba in no time. *Señor* Robles has my instructions to give you whatever you need. I'm at your full disposal if there's anything you might need that *Señor* Robles cannot help you with."

"Gracias, Licenciado," Pepe smiled.

They shook hands all around. Ortega gave Raymond a little bow.

"*Suerte, Doctor*," he said.

Raymond smiled back, not knowing what to say. *Suerte?*

"Follow me, *Señores*." Robles said. "Let's go have your passport pictures taken."

"I don't need to have my picture taken," Pepe said. "My Mexican passport is still good. Has another year to go."

"Let's get you a new one anyway." Robles shrugged. "You're here. Might as well."

Twenty minutes later, after a speedy and efficient tour of the facilities, where they had their pictures taken and all the necessary papers filled out, Pepe and Raymond emerged with two dark-green passports which testified to the world, without the shadow of a doubt, that they were native-born Mexicans from Oaxaca. Raymond's Mexican name was Ramón Robles de Parada; Pepe's name was Jose Luis Tapia Fernández.

"*Mucha suerte en Cuba*," Señor Robles told them, shaking both of their hands vigorously. "Have a very nice trip."

"*Gracias*," Raymond said.

Pepe nodded.

Pablo and Pedro waited outside exactly where they left them. Pedro smiled.

"To the hotel, *Señores*?" he asked.

"*Por favor*," Pepe replied. "*El Presidente*."

"I know."

Pedro held the car door open for them, and closed it after they went in. "*Vámonos rápido*," he told Pablo as he sat alongside him up front. "*Al hotel*."

The Mexicana plane that was to take them to Havana next day was thirty minutes late, so Raymond and Pepe used the time to browse around the myriad shops lining the airport corridors. Raymond's heart pounded in anticipation of the trip. He wondered what he would find in Cuba after all this time.

When they finally called the flight, he was immersed in childhood memories he thought forgotten. He tried to remember what the Rancho Boyeros airport in Havana looked like when he saw it last, but couldn't. Nowadays, he heard, it was called the José Martí airport.

"Let's board," Pepe said.

They handed their boarding passes to a smiling, dark-haired stewardess and went inside. Raymond breathed deeply, trying to quiet down his runaway heart.

"Relax," Pepe said. "Everything will be all right."

Despite its relative brevity, the flight seemed endless to Raymond. He was so uptight; he couldn't eat anything and only drank black coffee. Finally, the captain announced they were landing.

If Mexico City seemed brown, dirty and blurry from above, Havana looked blue-and-gold, clean and clear. There were certainly no traffic jams below that he could see – although Raymond did notice an inordinate number of bikers all over.

"Try to sound Mexican," Pepe told him as the plane taxied to a stop in the middle of the runway. "Watch your pronunciation."

"How do I sound Mexican?" Raymond asked, alarmed. "I've never lived in Mexico. I'm not familiar with the Mexican accents."

"Neither are the Cubans."

"Some Cubans are."

"Some, not all. Just try not to sound like a Cuban. I'm sure that will be enough." Pepe shrugged. "Speak at a slower tempo and don't move your hands too much."

Raymond's stomach knotted with apprehension as they deplaned. They approached immigration. A tall muscular man with a thin moustache, dressed in an olive-green uniform, greeted Raymond and asked to see his passport.

"*Buenos días,*" Raymond said, enunciating the words slowly.

The man had the rank of major, Raymond noticed. He recognized Pepe and his solemn face dissolved into a big, friendly smile.

"I see you're back, Pepe." He pointed at Raymond. "Who's your friend–"

"Ramón Robles de Parada." Pepe returned a warm smile and turned to face a dazzled Raymond. "Let me introduce you to Major Humberto Teceira."

"*Tanto Gusto.*" Raymond shook hands firmly with Teceira.

The major inspected Raymond's passport with curiosity, staring at the picture and then at Raymond.

"From Oaxaca, uh?" He asked. Like *Señor* Tapia here?"

"*Así es,*" Raymond forced himself to smile "Like him."

"You don't sound *Oaxaqueño.*" He shrugged, grinning. "But then neither does your friend Pepe."

"I beg your pardon?"

"You don't sound like from Oaxaca," the man said. "I studied in Mexico. I lived three years in Mexico City and one in Monterrey."

"He was raised in Mexico City, Humberto," Pepe explained. "As for me, I come to Cuba so often on business I probably have a Cuban accent now."

Teceira nodded to Pepe, then turned again toward Raymond.

"You don't sound like a *chilango* either."

"*Chilango?*" Raymond asked.

"Isn't that what you call people from Mexico City – *chilangos?*"

"Of course," Raymond said quickly. "I was just surprised you knew so much about my country."

"Lovely country, Mexico." The man stared at Raymond. "And so is Cuba. Welcome to Havana."

"*Gracias,*" Raymond said.

"Your passport is new," Teceira commented. You must do a lot of traveling, do you?"

"Some."

He inspected Raymond's passport again, flipping the pages back and forth. Raymond looked at Pepe. Teceira raised his head.

"I have a son named Ramón too, like you. He's your *tocayo.*" He grinned. "Your namesake."

Raymond smiled back. Not knowing what to say, he decided to say nothing.

"He's a doctor," Teceira said proudly. "What do you do?"

"I'm a doctor."

"Funny." Teceira shook his head with incredulity. "Both of you are doctors. You must meet my son while you're in Cuba."

"I'd love to."

"First time in Havana, Doctor?" Teceira asked.

"First time."

"Make sure you take him around, Pepe. Show him the sights."

"I intend to." Pepe's voice had an edge to it.

"I recommend seeing *La Cabana*, the Morro Castle and, of course, Varadero Beach – the most beautiful beach in the world. If you have more time, I would visit the *Valle de Vinales*. It's a beautiful place." He handed the passports back to them. "Have a pleasant stay in our country. How long will you be here for?"

"Two or three weeks, more or less," Pepe answered.

"You still in the sugar business?"

"Still in the sugar business."

"Where will you be staying in Havana, Pepe? The usual place?"

"Yes, at the *Habana Libre*."

"Nice hotel." Teceira smiled at Raymond. "A remnant of capitalism from the fifties, the old Havana Hilton. You'll like it, Doctor. Enjoy your stay."

"*Gracias*," Raymond said.

"I'll call on you at the hotel sometime, Pepe. Maybe we can have a drink together, and I can introduce my son to your friend."

"Sure."

"I'll look forward to it." Major Teceira smiled warmly.

As they walked through the bright corridors on the way to the exit, Raymond asked Pepe, "Sugar business? What was that all about?"

"My cover, Ramón. Everybody in Cuba might suspect I'm with the CIA, but I still need a cover. I buy Cuban sugar for a Mexican Consortium. Actually, I've gotten pretty good at it considering I didn't know anything about sugar when I started."

"I must admit I'm impressed," Raymond said. "There's never a dull moment with you, it seems. One moment you're with the CIA and the next you're a sugar buyer for a Mexican group."

"That's life, always changing." He grinned. "You know who that Major was?"

"No," Raymond answered. "But he sure asked a lot of questions."

"You really don't know who he was? You didn't guess?"

"No. Who is he?"

"He's Sonia's husband."

"What?" Raymond stopped abruptly, his stomach contracting into tight cold knots. "He's what?"

"Keep walking," Pepe told him. "I don't know what Major Teceira was doing here. Maybe he was checking airport operations. Or maybe he was checking *you* out. He's the head of national security, reporting directly to Raul Castro, the defense minister."

"How come you didn't tell me this before, Pepe?"

"I didn't want to make you any more nervous than you were

already. Besides, I couldn't. He was with us the whole time."

"I'm sure nervous now." Raymond let his breath out. "Do you think Teceira suspects anything?"

"I think it may have been a coincidence," Pepe said. "Teceira comes to the airport all the time to check on arriving flights. Relax, Ramón. Let things just flow. The worst part is over. You are inside Cuba."

Raymond sighed loudly, opening his eyes wide and making a funny face. "All I need now is to get out in one piece."

Outside, the day was getting hotter. They hired an old taxi to take them to the hotel. It was a dark-blue relic from the fifties, without hubcaps or air-conditioning, and with bald tires. The driver was a short young man with curly black hair.

"My name's Mauricio," he told them. "Are you *turistas*?"

"Yes, we're tourists," Pepe replied.

"You have old jeans you don't want?" he asked them. "Throwaway clothes you don't like? Shirts, underwear, anything? How about old shoes?"

"Nothing," Pepe answered.

"Too bad. My feet are about the same size as yours," he told Raymond. "Look at my soles, see? You see the big holes? You sure you don't have an old pair of shoes with you? I'd really appreciate it if you do."

"Maybe," Raymond said. "I'll look when we stop."

"*Gracias, Señor*," the driver said happily. "Where are you from?"

"Mexico."

"Nice place, Mexico." He whistled gaily, probably thinking of his new shoes. "Though I prefer Miami. I hear Miami is very nice, like Havana used to be. You know Miami, *Señor*?"

"Yes."

"Is it nice?"

"Very nice."

The old Havana Hilton hadn't changed much, Raymond decided. It had just gotten older. The magnificent entrance was the same he remembered – with the unique dome inside which Raymond likened to a turtle-shell the first time he saw it as a kid.

"Nothing has changed here," Raymond told Pepe with a nostalgic sigh. "Not that I can see, anyway."

"Nothing has changed anywhere," Pepe said, breathing heavily from carrying his luggage. "Let's check in and go to *Las Canitas* on the second floor for a drink. Remember *Las Canitas?*"

"Vaguely."

"You'll remember it better after this trip." Pepe laughed. "They prepare the best *mojitos* in town after *La Floridita.*"

"See you there in ten minutes."

As Raymond washed his face, stripped from the waist up, there was a knock on the door. He went to open, thinking it was the maid.

A very attractive blonde green-eyed woman in a turquoise dress that had seen better days stood smiling in front of the door. She seemed vaguely familiar.

"Yes?" he asked, smiling. "What can I do for–"

He stopped, recognizing her, and his heart fluttered. Pepe had been wrong. She looked prettier than thirty years ago.

It was Sonia.

CHAPTER III

Raymond's first impulse was to embrace and kiss Sonia, but the years of unfamiliarity and his own cautious personality held him back. Sonia, however, felt no such compunction. With the same carefree laugh and unrestrained ebullience he remembered when they were teenagers, she wrapped him in a bear hug and kissed him smack on the cheek. She smelled of herbs, perfume and nostalgia.

"Come in, Sonia," he said, embarrassed, checking for curious onlookers down the hall – he found none. "*Por favor.*"

She entered the room. He closed the door behind her, sighing with relief. Sonia stared at him, a big smile on her face.

"Let me look at you, Ramoncito!" she said, using the name she used to call him when they were kids. She stepped back, appraising him. "You're in great shape. You must do a lot of exercise, do you?"

Raymond felt even more embarrassed. Only his mother and Sonia had ever called him Ramoncito – and to be inspected by Sonia like that was, to say the least, unnerving. His face burned.

"I jog every morning at six wherever I am," he replied mechanically as he searched for a shirt. "Do karate three times a week. Play tennis whenever I can."

"You look great!" she exclaimed. "You still have a marvelous body and all your hair. You really haven't changed much."

"Neither have you, Sonia."

She laughed, pleased, throwing her head back in a gesture he remembered well. A network of fine wrinkles appeared around her eyes and mouth, and suddenly Raymond was eighteen again. He felt like kissing Sonia.

"I've put on a little weight since we used to go to the club together," she said. "And I have to dye my hair to keep it blonde. Otherwise I feel fine. Remember the club?"

"I do."

"We spent some good times there, didn't we?"

The Profesionales Club, which Sonia and Raymond used to refer to simply as 'the club,' was where they had made love for the first time the night of his high school graduation dance. A poignant memory of that moment, long forgotten, rushed into his mind with vivid detail.

"Yes, we did," he replied. "What's happened to it?"

"Still there. They turned it into a government office."

"Too bad."

"I agree." She laughed. "I work there."

"Really? And what do you do?"

"I'm the director of hospital administration. I manage the hospital network in the island."

"That's a pretty important position, isn't it?"

"It is." Sonia nodded. "And it isn't. Unfortunately, there isn't much to manage."

"What do you mean?"

"No money. Our hospitals have a very limited budget and practically no medicines and no equipment. It's sad." Sonia sighed, and then smiled again brightly. "But let's not be sad tonight. It's a happy occasion that you have returned to Cuba."

In spite of himself, Raymond had become increasingly more aware of Sonia's nearness. Her perfume tingled his skin. As she talked, she brushed her hand accidentally against his chest, sending a shiver through his body. He wanted so much to hold her against him and kiss her. He wondered what her full lips would taste like after so many years. *Would they be familiar?* he thought.

He realized they were still standing. He motioned to the couch.

"Please, sit down," he said.

"Just for a minute."

"What about your personal life, Sonia?" Raymond changed the subject, trying to still his heart. "Are you happy?"

Sonia leaned back, looking perplexed.

"What a question, Ramón." She pondered a moment. "Let's say I'm satisfied. Are *you* happy, Ramón?"

"No." He shrugged. "I recently lost my wife."

"Did you love her very much?"

"Yes."

She sighed.

"I can understand that," she said. "Are you seeing anyone now?"

"No." He paused. "You?"

"I have a husband."

He nodded, his heart contracting suddenly.

"Yes, of course," he said.

"I've been with him thirty-two years, ever since you left and went to the United States to live. He's a good man. He's not perfect – but he's a good man."

"You love him, Sonia?"

"He's a good man," she repeated.

Raymond breathed deeply, his heart racing again.

"I don't want to do anything to hurt him," Sonia said sadly, as if reading his thoughts. "He doesn't deserve it."

Raymond remained quiet, his mind a rising cacophony of contradictory thoughts and feelings and desires.

"I understand," he said to fill the unbearable screaming silence. "I do."

"You and I can be friends, though." She smiled, her mood changing again. "After all, you're the father of my only son."

"I'd like that very much."

"Me too."

She leaned forward and kissed him lightly and tenderly on the cheek. Her smell enveloped him. He didn't move.

"For a long time, I missed you terribly," she said, smiling sadly. "You left me hurt, pregnant and alone. I resented it. I hated you!"

"I'm sorry."

"What do you know? It's easy to say 'I'm sorry' after thirty years. It's a lot harder to live through it."

"Please, tell me about it. I want to know." She sat on the edge of the sofa. He didn't move.

"My parents kicked me out. You know how traditional they were."

"Oh, my God. I didn't know."

"There are many things you don't know."

"True." He lowered his head.

"Humberto was my only support. I met him at the *milicia* one day,

31

working in the sugar cane field to help the revolution. He was kind and gentle, someone to talk to. I told him about you. I told him I was pregnant. He listened. He's a great listener, Humberto. We talked for hours after work. One day he offered to marry me."

She stopped, her eyes wet with tears. Raymond wanted so much to hug her but didn't dare do it. He was afraid he would lose control.

"I said no," she continued. "He tried to convice me. He said it would be better for my child. He told me he loved me, that with time I would learn to love him. I kept saying no."

"Did you?"

"Did I what?"

"Did you learn to love him?"

"I've only loved one man in my life," she said.

Raymond said nothing. He felt hot and uncomfortable.

"I never married Humberto – I couldn't." Sonia's eyes were bright. "But I moved in with him, and Mon was born two months later. He filled my life with joy. I devoted my life to him. I never had another child – I didn't want to."

"So you're not really married." Hope flowered again within Raymond's agitated chest.

"It's almost the same thing," Sonia said. "I've been living with Humberto ever since."

"Why did you name your son Ramón?"

"I'm a hopeless romantic," she said, smiling. "It was a way to remember you, I guess."

"Humberto didn't mind?"

"Humberto can be such an understanding and caring soul when he wants to – he said nothing."

"What about your parents? What happened to them?"

"The fact I didn't marry Humberto really hurt them. They never talked to me again. They left to Miami on the Mariel boatlift. I hear from them through Pepe from time to time. They never forgave me."

"I'm sorry."

"It's easy for you to say you're sorry, Ramoncito. You say 'I'm sorry' a lot. Did you ever stop to think about whether you really mean it or not?"

"I'm really sor–" he started and stopped, feeling himself blush.

"See what I mean?" She laughed.

Raymond made a face, attempting a feeble smile.

"You had the same expression when we were kids."

"Really?"

She nodded, smiling at him.

"I met Humberto today at the airport," he said.

"I know."

"You *know*?"

"He went there to meet you." Sonia smiled. "He wanted to know what you looked like."

"He knows about me then?"

"Of course, he's not stupid. He knew you were coming."

"So he knows I'm not Mexican?"

"Of course."

Raymond's mouth dropped open. His mind raced.

"He *knows*, Sonia? That's pretty dangerous for me – and for Pepe."

"Don't worry," Sonia said. "Humberto won't say or do anything. Besides, even if he wanted to, he wouldn't. He loves his son – and me – too much."

"*His* son?"

"It's his son too." Sonia turned serious. "After all, he raised Mon."

"That's true." Raymond clasped and unclasped his hands nervously. "He's also with the government, and he knows I entered Cuba with a fake Mexican passport. He could get me thrown into a Cuban jail in the blinking of an eye – and he has the power to do it too."

"He won't turn you in."

"I wish I could be so sure. He might think I'm a CIA spy or something – after all, I'm an American citizen."

"I give you my word nothing is going to happen to you – not because of Humberto, anyway."

"I don't know how you can be so sure."

"Trust me."

"Why do I have the feeling, ever since I met Pepe in Miami, I'm not being told everything?"

"Who knows?" Sonia grinned at him. "Maybe you're psychic."

"Why did Humberto come to the airport this morning and put me through the third-degree instead of letting you or Ramón introduce us?"

"That's the way Humberto is. He likes to be in control of the situation."

"He sure was in total control at the airport. He asked me a lot of questions too – on purpose, just to irritate me."

"You can't blame him, can you?"

"I guess not." Raymond shrugged. "When do I get to meet my *son?*"

"Right now. He's downstairs with Pepe at *Las Canitas*, waiting for you."

Inside *Las Canitas* the temperature was warm, and the light was dim. Flickering candles in red glass holders illuminated the small mostly-empty round tables covered with white tablecloths scattered around the room. The massive bar in the middle, constructed of solid mahogany, was round too. A five-man combo on a small platform played an old familiar *bolero* Raymond knew well; he had danced it with Sonia many times.

He was overwhelmed with reminiscences. Forgotten memories invaded his consciousness with chaotic flashes – the way Sonia looked the first time they made love, the deep-green color of the sea at Santa María del Mar beach, the smell of jasmine. Raymond felt like a teenager growing up in Cuba again.

They spotted Pepe right away. He sat in front of the combo. Next to him sat a tall young man, looking uncomfortable in a shiny, dark-blue suit.

As they reached the table, the young man rose. Pepe stood too. For a moment, the four people looked at each other in an awkward silence. Then Sonia spoke.

"This is your father, Mon," she said quietly.

Raymond's knees were weak; his heart pounded so hard, he wondered if the others could hear it.

"*Qué tal el viaje?*" Mon asked, smiling politely. "You had a good trip?"

"Fine," Raymond replied. "Somewhat uneventful, but fine."

"I'm glad."

The similarities between them were striking. The color of Mon's eyes and his smile, he inherited from Sonia; everything else – height, color, shape – he inherited from Raymond.

Raymond had the unsettling feeling of looking at himself in the mirror, twenty years earlier.

Major Teceira must have seen the uncanny resemblance at the airport too. There was no denying that *Doctor* Ramón Teceira was Raymond's son.

"Why don't you ask your father to sit down, Mon?" Pepe chuckled. "We'll be more comfortable."

"Excuse me." Mon gave Pepe a sharp look. "Please sit down." He made room for them at the table. "*Mamá*, sit here, so you can be next to... next to..." He flushed, not knowing how to address Raymond.

Pepe came to Mon's rescue.

"How about a drink?" he asked genially, a big smile on his face. "This is a special occasion. What would you like, Sonia? A *mojito* maybe? They make great *mojitos* here."

"A *mojito* is fine." Sonia laughed. "This is a special occasion indeed. We must celebrate Ramoncito's visit."

"And his meeting Mon."

"*And* his meeting Mon."

"You want a *mojito* too, Ramón?" Pepe asked.

"*Por favor*, Pepe," Raymond replied. "Let's celebrate. It's been a long time."

"Thirty-two years exactly," Sonia reminded him. "That's how long it's been."

Pepe ordered the drinks. Mon glanced at Raymond.

"You look younger than I expected," he said.

"What did you expect?"

"I don't know." He fumbled for the right word to say. "Someone older, I guess."

"Sorry to disappoint you."

The drinks arrived, and the waiter distributed them around the table.

"What brings you to Cuba?" Mon asked Raymond, who thought he hadn't heard right.

"Excuse me?"

"What brings you to Cuba?"

"You."

"Me?" Mon's voice sounded surprised. "You didn't come to see me in thirty-two years. Why now?"

"*Salud!*" Pepe toasted, interrupting them. "To fathers, sons, freedom, and all things beautiful."

Raymond and Mon sipped from their drinks, staring at each other.

"We need to talk, son," Raymond said.

"Don't call me son. You're not my father. I don't even carry your name. My real father is Humberto Teceira, the man who raised me."

"I realize you must be sore with me," Raymond said. "You must understand I knew nothing about you till last week. It's not that I didn't want to be your father – it's that I didn't know you were my son."

"The fact is that you left my mother pregnant."

"I didn't know she was pregnant "

"For you to be able to leave so easily, you obviously didn't love her very much."

"Not true. I asked her to come with me. She said no."

"Maybe you didn't sound very convincing."

"I tried, believe me. She didn't want to come."

"Why did you have to come back into our lives after all this time?" Mon's voice cracked. "Why did you have to come to Cuba and stir things up again?"

Raymond stared at Pepe and Sonia helplessly. They pretended to be listening to the music.

"To see you," Raymond replied. "Because you asked me to come."

"I asked you to come?"

"I understand how you must feel, son," Raymond said softly. "I'm a doctor too, remember? It's not easy to accept dying. I'm awfully sorry for you, believe me."

"Dying? Who in hell told you I'm dying?"

"Hello, everyone," a familiar mocking voice said, startling Raymond. "I see you've met my son already, *Doctor*. I'm glad."

A hush fell on the table as they stared at the newcomer. Major Teceira bent down and kissed Sonia on the cheek. The combo finished playing a tune Raymond wasn't sure he knew, although it sounded somewhat familiar. A few hands clapped, and then silence permeated the room.

Raymond stood, forcing himself to smile pleasantly at the visitor.

"*Buenas noches*, Major Teceira," he said. "Please join us. I believe you know everyone at this table."

Mon offered the major an empty chair. Major Teceira sat down solemnly. The combo started playing again, a *bolero* Raymond definitely didn't know.

CHAPTER IV

"My Mexican friend." Major Teceira smiled pleasantly. "I'm happy to see you enjoy Cuban *mojitos*. You do like your *mojito*, don't you, *Doctor*?"

"It's very nice," Raymond replied guardedly.

"You know what it is, Doctor?" Teceira leaned toward Raymond, raising an eyebrow. "It's the ground *hierba buena* in it. That's what gives the *mojito* its taste."

"I see."

"Do you like them better than *margaritas*?" Teceira's voice had a sharp mocking tone that didn't escape Raymond. "Or you don't like *margaritas*? They're the Mexican national drink, aren't they?"

"I like *margaritas*."

"But you do like *mojitos* better, don't you, doctor?"

"I–"

"Stop it, *Papá*!" Mon said abruptly, interrupting Raymond. "That's enough!"

"Yes, Humberto," Sonia said. "*Ya está bien* – enough is enough!"

Raymond looked from one to the other, not understanding fully but beginning to comprehend.

"Let's cut out this idiotic farce, Humberto," Pepe joined the others. "It's not fair to Ramón."

Raymond eyed Pepe, finally understanding. He turned to face his son. "You're *not* dying of cancer, are you, Mon?"

"No."

"You're not ill either, are you?"

"Not according to my last checkup three weeks ago," Mon replied. "I was declared in perfect health then."

"I see."

Raymond stared at Pepe, seething with anger. He took a deep

38

breath, trying to maintain control. He couldn't remember being so angry ever. His heart pounded, and he could hardly breathe.

"It was the only way I could bring you to Cuba, Ramón," Pepe spoke. "Forgive me – but I needed you here. It was terribly important."

"For whom?" Raymond's voice had a sharp, cutting edge. "For you or for me?"

"For both of us, I hope."

"You tricked me, Pepe." Raymond said angrily. "You *all* tricked me. I hope you had a good time, Sonia."

"I'm sorry, Ramoncito."

Sonia lowered her head. Raymond turned to Pepe again.

"You lied to me, Pepe."

"Only partially, Ramón. Many of the things I told are true."

"Which, for instance?"

"Mon *is* your son."

"But he doesn't want to see me, and he's not dying of cancer."

"He's not," Pepe said tiredly, suddenly looking old and wrinkled beyond his years. "I am."

"I beg your pardon?" Raymond was dazed.

"Mon's not dying of cancer," Pepe said slowly. "I am."

"You are?" Raymond's mind raced. "I'm getting more confused by the minute, Pepe. Now you're dying of cancer. Are you really dying of cancer, Pepe, or is this another lie?"

"I'm not lying to you, Ramón. I swear." Pepe raised his right hand. "I *am* dying of cancer. It's the God's truth."

Raymond gazed at his friend with narrowed eyes. Pepe gave him a sad smile, shrugging fatalistically.

"I know you don't believe me, Ramón," he said, "but everything I told you about your son was true – only about myself."

Pepe's face was contrite. It conveyed sincerity to Raymond.

"I do believe you," Raymond finally said. "I'm sorry, Pepe."

"Don't be, Ramón. We all have to go sometime. It's my turn now."

"I'm sorry, anyway."

"*Gracias*." Pepe swallowed. "I appreciate your concern. It means a lot to me."

The band started playing a fast song. It was the first fast song they played all night, and it broke the emotionally charged mood.

"Tell me why I am in Cuba, Pepe," Raymond said quietly. Why did you bring me here? Why did you trick me into coming to Havana? What do you *want* from me?"

There was silence at the table. They all looked at each other.

"We'll explain everything to you," Pepe said softly. "Let's go up to my room. It's more private. We don't want strange ears overhearing what we have to tell you. Besides, someone wants to meet you."

"Who?"

"Someone you know."

"Someone I know? Who?"

"You'll see." Pepe smiled.

They sat around Pepe's room quietly – Sonia, Teceira and Mon on the large burnt-orange sofa, Pepe on the bed, and Raymond on one of the two matching armchairs. A soft sea breeze blew the sheer white-cotton curtains away from the large picture window, refreshing the warm room. The hotel air-conditioned system either didn't work or was disconnected to save electricity.

"What's going on here, Pepe?" Raymond asked. "I demand an explanation."

"You'll have it," Pepe replied. "We'll tell you everything."

"Don't lie to me anymore, please, Pepe," Raymond said. "I've heard enough lies during the last three days to last me a lifetime."

"No lies." Pepe gestured with his hand. "I promise."

Pepe cleared his throat. Sonia lowered her eyes and inspected her nails. Mon and Teceira watched Pepe.

"We brought you here under false pretenses because we need you."

"So you said before," Raymond said. "What do you need me for?"

"What I'm about to tell you may sound weird to you, Ramón," Pepe said. "Perhaps even crazy. Promise me, before I start, you'll listen to me till the end."

"Is it so crazy?"

"It might sound to you that way, Ramoncito," Sonia said softly. "You're a very logical man – and this is anything but logical."

"Although it does have a logic to it." Teceira chuckled. "In fact, you may find the entire thing very logical."

"What is it, damn you?" Raymond's voice was hoarse. "What in hell do you want from me?"

Pepe exchanged glances with Teceira and the others, a puzzled expression on his face. "What happened to our visitor?" He asked them.

"He's late, as usual." Teceira shrugged. "You know how he is."

"Who are we waiting for?" Raymond asked.

"The person we told you about," Pepe said. "We would like for him to be here before we tell you about all this."

"It's a man then?"

"*Sí.*"

"*Quién es*, Pepe?" Raymond asked. "Who is he?"

"You'll know soon enough," Pepe replied. "He's the central part in all this. We would like for him to tell you himself."

"You're really making a melodrama out of this, Pepe." Raymond laughed mirthlessly. "This sounds like a television soap opera

"I know it." Pepe laughed too, and the others chorused. "But that's the way he wanted it. He's the boss. All of us in this room, in one way or another, work for him."

"All?" Raymond asked.

"All." Pepe smiled. "Mon, for instance, is his personal physician."

Raymond looked at his son, who nodded silently. He glanced at Sonia next.

"You work for this man too, Sonia?" Sonia smiled at him, nodding.

"And you, Teceira?"

Teceira nodded silently too.

"Who's this man, Pepe?" Raymond asked.

As if on cue, there was a knock on the door. Pepe stood. "That must be him," he said. "See for yourself, Ramón." Pepe opened the door. A tall bearded man entered the room, followed by two men dressed in olive-green army uniforms carrying brown shopping bags.

"I brought a couple of bottles of Havana Club, and all the ingredients to make *mojitos*," the man said loudly, a big charismatic smile on his face. "Might as well drink something while we talk."

Raymond recognized the man instantly, and his mouth dropped

41

open with surprise. Everyone in the room rose respectfully. Raymond rose too, on unsteady legs.

The man shook hands all around and kissed Sonia on the cheek. He walked toward Raymond and offered his hand to him.

"So you're the man who's going to do it, uh?" he said, shaking hands with Raymond. "I've heard a lot about you, *Doctor* Peters."

He laughed loudly, tilting his head sideways in a characteristic gesture. Raymond had seen it often on the television news and the movies.

The man was Fidel Castro.

CHAPTER V

Raymond plopped on his chair, staring at Fidel Castro. His heart thrashed, and his knees trembled. Exhaling slowly, he tried to calm down. This trip to Cuba was becoming more surprising by the second.

"What's going on here?" he asked. "I want an explanation."

The bearded man laughed heartily, as if Raymond had told him a very funny joke. His face crisscrossed with wrinkles. Everyone in the room laughed too.

"We'll give you one," he said. "But let's have some *mojitos* and relax first. I never get a chance to relax in this country anymore. It's only work, work, and work. It's worse than living in the United States. This isn't *Gringolandia* here. This is Cuba. You work a lot yourself, Ramón? You don't mind if I call you Ramón, do you? I can't get myself to call you Raymond. After all, you're Cuban."

"No." Raymond was dazed by the torrent of words. "I don't mind."

"You can call me Fidel."

Raymond nodded. Castro in person was much like Castro on television – the only person who talked was he.

"Come with me to the kitchen, Ramón." Castro put an arm around Raymond's shoulders. "Let's go make some *mojitos* ourselves. I don't want to sound like I'm bragging, but I make the best *mojitos* in town – better than *La Floridita* or *La Bodeguita del Medio* or anywhere. You watch, and you'll learn my secret, Ramón. You'll go back home as the best *mojito* maker in the United States. Here, have a cigar."

Castro stopped abruptly, pulled two cigars from his shirt pocket and offered one to Raymond. In the sudden silence, Raymond heard Sonia's muted laugh and the strident sound of an insistent car horn down on the street.

"*No, gracias*," Raymond said.

Castro lit his cigar and puffed from it. Raymond watched the match flame expand and contract with each puff. It made Castro's face red.

"Ahhh," Castro gurgled with pleasure, exhaling the aromatic smoke toward the ceiling. "Why don't you have a cigar, Ramón? These are the best Havana cigars anywhere. They're hand rolled especially for me."

"I don't smoke, *Señor* Castro."

"Call me Fidel, I told you. I hate formalities." Words started tumbling out of Castro's mouth again, obliterating for Raymond all other sounds. "Come help me with the *mojitos*, Ramón. That way we can talk too. You like jokes, Ramón? All Cubans like jokes. I heard a good one the other day. These three generals meet in the Middle East – a Russian, an American and a Cuban–"

He pushed open the swinging doors to the small white kitchenette. Raymond missed terribly the cool green environment of his operating room back in Palm Beach. Undermining people's skins and making noses perfect was infinitely more fun to him than listening to endless monologues – even if the person who voiced them was Fidel Castro.

Raymond wondered what he was *really* doing in Cuba. Although Castro's skin was beginning to sag, it didn't seem likely he wanted plastic surgery.

Castro's aides had laid out carefully all the *mojito* ingredients on the scarred yellow formica top of the kitchen table. There were six bottles of Havana Club Añejo rum, a large pile of *hierba buena*, lemons, a container with sugar, and a large bag of ice.

"I prepared *mojitos* for Hemingway and, afterwards, he preferred mine to anybody else's," Castro continued his nonstop conversation, puffing on his cigar. "Papá acknowledged to me one night I made them better than at *La Floridita* – and you must know, Ramón, how difficult to please Hemingway was! It's my own special recipe. Everyone thinks it's the rum, but it's not – it's how you mix it. I can make *mojitos* with any rum, and they will taste good. You know how to make *mojitos*, Ramón?"

"No."

"What about Hemingway? Did you ever meet him?"

"No, sir."

"*Fidel*, Ramón." Castro stopped puffing on his cigar for an instant to look at Raymond. "Call me Fidel."

"Fidel."

"That's better." He resumed puffing, as he deftly started mixing the drinks, enveloping both of them in a cloud of smoke. "I want to get to know you well. I want us to be comrades. The fact you're a capitalist, and I'm a communist doesn't mean we can't be friends. I hear you're one of the top plastic surgeons in the world. No wonder your son is so talented."

"You know my son well, Fidel?"

"Well enough to trust him with my life. He's my personal physician. He's been my physician now for how long?" He counted fingers. "Is it two or three years? I can't remember. It seems like forever. He started out as my cardiologist and ended up as the only doctor I trust in this country – how do you like that?"

Castro pushed open the swinging doors.

"Hey, Mon!" he called. "Mon! Come here a minute, will you?"

Mon arrived, smiling.

"Yes, Fidel."

"How long have you been my personal physician?"

"Over three years, Fidel. Why?"

"I was telling your father, and I couldn't remember." He turned his back on Mon and continued fussing over the drinks. "*Gracias.*"

"*Eso era todo*, Fidel?"

"That was all."

"*Me voy para que sigan hablando, entonces.*"

Mon left as quickly as he had come.

"I'm afraid I'm a terrible patient," Castro said as he adorned the row of tall glasses with *hierba buena*. "It makes your son insane."

"Why?"

"Why?" Castro laughed. "Because I never do anything he tells me to do, that's why. Does he get angry! He has a temper, your son. Do you have a temper too?"

"If I'm provoked."

"Let's not provoke you then." Castro took a step back and admired his creation approvingly. "There, I'm finished. Grab a glass, Ramón. You're going to taste the best *mojito* in the world, bar none. Go ahead, drink!"

Castro took one of the tall glasses, and Raymond did the same.

They sipped from their drinks. Raymond couldn't taste any difference between Castro's *mojitos* and those he drank at the bar.

"Wonderful, don't you agree?" Fidel beamed with pleasure. "I must have been a bartender in another incarnation. Tell me the truth, Ramón. Isn't this the best *mojito* you ever tasted, Ramón? Isn't it?"

Without waiting for an answer, Castro trampled back into the living room. It was hard to keep up with him, Raymond decided. Castro was a man in perpetual motion. Raymond followed him.

"Grab a glass, everybody!" he cried at the others. "Drink up and be happy. The *mojitos* are ready. This is like in *gringolandia* today – self-service. I told Venancio and Ramiro to wait outside, so we could have more privacy. Hurry up! I want to toast to our guest."

Obediently, they all trudged to the kitchen and reemerged with glasses on their hands. Standing side-by-side, big smiles on their faces, Raymond noticed for the first time how remarkably alike Castro and Pepe were. They were similar in height, body weight and facial characteristics. If it weren't because Pepe was shaved and balding, and Castro had a beard, they could pass for twins.

"To Ramón." Castro lifted his glass, and the others did the same. "The man who's going to operate on us and change our lives, Pepe."

"To Ramón," they chorused.

Raymond's grip loosened on his glass, and his *mojito* tumbled to the floor. It rolled on the threadbare carpet, spilling its contents. In one swift motion, Sonia retrieved the glass. Raymond's hands were shaking.

"I'm going to do what?" Raymond asked slowly. He was beginning to understand what he was doing in Cuba.

"You're going to perform plastic surgery on us," Fidel replied, smiling. "That's why you're here. Didn't you want to know? You want another *mojito*, Ramón?"

"No, thank you."

"Have one, you'll need it." He took Teceira's glass from his hand and handed it to Raymond. "It'll do you good."

Mechanically, his mind racing, Raymond took a long pull of his drink. Ice and fire slid down his throat.

"How is it?" Castro asked. "Good?"

"Very good."

"I'll explain it to you in simple terms," Castro said. "You're going to operate me, so I look like Pepe; and you're going to operate Pepe, so he looks like me."

"I didn't come here to operate on anybody."

"You came here to operate on us."

"I have no instruments and no assistants

"We have all the instruments you need," Mon said. "Maybe better than what you have in the United States. We're not Indians here, *father*." He pronounced the word 'father' as if he had said 'shit.' "Cuban medicine is among the finest in the world. I'll be your assistant. I'm a trained cardiologist and anesthesiologist. Isn't that good enough for you?"

"This is crazy, son!" Raymond shouted, losing control. "We're not talking Mexican tortillas here."

"We told you it might sound crazy to you at first." Pepe smiled, making a childish face at Raymond. "But it will make a lot of sense to you later."

"Why would you want me to make you look like Fidel, Pepe?" Raymond asked. "Explain that one to me. Are you going to stay in Cuba as Castro?"

"I am."

"I see." Raymond's mind worked rapidly. "Are you leaving Cuba, Fidel?"

Castro nodded, puffing on his cigar.

"Don't say it so loud," he said. "Someone might hear you."

"Don't tell me you're going back with me to Mexico?"

"Right again."

"And this parody has been set up jointly by you, the CIA and the Mexican government. Isn't that right, Fidel?"

"How smart you are, Ramón." Castro beamed approvingly, blowing smoke over Raymond's head at the ceiling. "You're unraveling the entire plot in front of our very eyes."

"What I don't understand is why?"

"Guess again, Ramón," Castro said placidly. "You're doing great so far."

"Why would you want to leave Cuba?" Raymond asked. "There might be several possible reasons – it's dangerous for you here, you're tired of all the problems and want to retire, you feel you have done all you can and can't do any more, you're sick."

"Bingo!" Castro exclaimed. "All of the above."

"What's wrong with you physically, Fidel?" Raymond asked.

"I have a heart condition which your cardiologist son has detected. He says I need to slow down, or I may die."

Raymond searched his son's eyes for an explanation.

"Acute angina and hypertension," Ramón said

"What would you do in Mexico, Fidel?" Raymond asked.

"*Nada.*"

"Nothing?"

"Practically nothing. Relax, mostly. I'll settle in Oaxaca, or maybe Mérida, under the assumed name of Jose Orozco, and write my memoirs."

"And you, Pepe?"

"This is my opportunity to do something for my country, Ramón." Pepe grinned. "I'm dying, anyway. My doctor says I'll last nine months. Suppose I get to live a year, or maybe two. I'll have twelve months or more to turn Cuba into a democratic country again."

"This is sheer lunacy," Raymond said, looking from one to the other. "How do you intend to do all this?"

"Please, sit down, Ramón," Castro said gently. "We'll explain our plan to you."

CHAPTER VI

"We'll fake an automobile accident in Varadero," Castro explained, puffing on his cigar. "Teceira will take care of the details. I'll be on a visit to check out beachfront erosion, or something like that. Pepe will be in the car with me. We'll be rushed to the hospital where you'll perform the operation. That's when Pepe and I will switch identities."

"I haven't even examined you yet," Raymond protested. "Didn't you say you were sick? I may not be able to operate on you. I don't want you to die on the operating table."

"That's a chance you and I will have to take, I guess."

"What about Pepe? He's sick too. I need to check both of you."

"Start checking then," Castro said. "We're at your disposal."

"It's not that simple." Raymond sighed with frustration. "What about the facilities we'll use? Who'll be there to assist us, Ramón?"

"No one, I'm afraid. We thought it would be too risky to involve anyone else. You and I will do it all. You'll perform the surgery; I'll handle the anesthesia and help you with the operation."

"Have you done surgery before, Ramón?"

"Maybe more than you, *father*. I've done dozens of open-heart operations, and, as I told you, I'm a trained anesthesiologist. I'll bring with me all types of medicines in case we run into trouble."

"We need somebody else."

"I can help," Sonia said. "I'm a trained nurse."

Mon questioned Raymond with his eyes and then made an approving face.

"All right," Raymond said after a pause. "What about the facilities themselves, Mon? Are they suitable? What do they look like? Where are they located?"

"Half a mile away from where the accident will take place," Mon replied. "They're makeshift hospital facilities under a tent in the

49

country. We use them to provide checkups and minor surgery to the locals. This one has been equipped specially. Everything is state of the art inside – I told you before. One thing we have in Cuba is good doctors – and excellent medical equipment."

"You just don't have electricity or medicines," Raymond said sharply. "Not good for obtaining optimum results during surgery."

"We have everything we need for *this* surgery."

"So you say."

"You'll have to take my word for it, *father*."

"I don't take anybody's word when it comes to a surgery, Mon. I'm responsible for the lives of my patients." Raymond turned to Castro. "Let's get something else clear here, Fidel. You may be in charge of this country, but if I accept to do it – which I don't know yet – I'll be in total control of this surgery. That's non-negotiable. Do you understand me, Fidel?"

"Do I seem mentally deficient to you, Ramón?"

"Don't play games with me, Fidel. Yes or no! Do you understand me?"

"Yes."

"Do you accept it?"

Castro stared at Raymond with smoldering eyes. He finally nodded. "Yes."

"Good. As soon as we get to Varadero, I'll check out the equipment myself." He addressed Ramón. "And we'll check out Pepe and Fidel. I don't want any surprises in the operating room."

"Fine."

"What other problems can we have here, Fidel?" Raymond asked. "What do you mean, Ramón?"

"I mean problems that could affect the success of the surgery."

"I don't understand you, Ramón," Castro said. "I really don't."

"What about suspicion from others – such as relatives, friends or acquaintances?" Raymond inquired. "Anyone you're worried about?"

"The only person I'm worried about is my brother, Raul. He's got a suspicious mind." Castro smiled. "So I've taken the precaution to send him to Russia on an urgent mission. He'll be in Moscow tied up for three to four weeks. That will give us enough time for the tissues to heal and the stitches to be removed, isn't that true, *Doctor*?"

"Depends on your skin – and Pepe's," Raymond replied curtly. "I would've preferred six weeks. I suppose, under the circumstances, three to four weeks will have to do. But I don't like it."

"You don't have to like it, Ramón," Castro said. "Will you do it?"

"Do I have a choice, Fidel?"

Castro smiled pleasantly. It was better to have Castro talking than quiet, Raymond decided.

"You have a choice, Ramón," Castro replied. "But I wouldn't recommend it."

"If I don't do it, Teceira will throw me in jail or worse – is that it, Fidel?"

"You got it right," Teceira grinned. "I'd like that very much too – for many reasons. However, I must say I'd be terribly disappointed not to be able to carry out this mission as we planned it – and, consequently, irritable. It would mean we wasted a lot of time with you. We'd have to find somebody else suitable, change the logistics once more, and arrange for Raul to be out of the country again. I'll be very irritable."

"And Teceira turns into an ogre when he gets irritable," Castro chortled. "*Un verdadero ogro.* You should see how he gets when his lunch isn't ready on time."

"You're damn right!" Teceira cried. "I'll throw you in jail so fast, you won't know what hit you, doctor." He snapped his fingers at Raymond for effect. "Like this!"

"On what charge?" Raymond asked. "Wait, Teceira, don't tell me. Let me guess. How about an American spy with a fake Mexican passport? Don't you shoot spies in Cuba?"

"You got it right again, doctor." Teceira's smile seemed more like a grimace.

"You're so bright, Ramón." Castro chuckled. "I'm impressed. You understand things so clearly and so rapidly. I'm delighted we chose you to do the surgery."

"I wish I could say the same."

"Look at it this way, Ramón," Castro said amiably. "You'll be doing the right thing, as far as we're concerned – and it will be interesting."

"No question about it, Fidel."

51

"You really don't have much of a choice."

"One question for you, Pepe," Raymond said. "Fidel has a mane of hair, and you're balding. I can do your face, but I can't do your hair on such short notice – the hair transplant wouldn't look good. How do you intend to solve your hair problem?"

Without answering, Pepe fetched the black bag he had hand-carried since Miami and tossed it on the bed. He opened it and started emptying out its contents. Raymond saw a blue jogging suit fly out, followed by tennis shoes, t-shirts, underwear, several shirts.

"Ahhh," Pepe said finally. "Here they are."

He picked up the bag, opened it wide and showed inside to Raymond.

"Look, Ramón. This is how I intend to do it."

The bag was full of hair, the same gray color as Castro's.

"What is it, Pepe?" Raymond asked. "All I see is hair."

"Not hair, Ramón, wigs!" Pepe replied. "Twelve custom-made wigs, one for every month of the year – if I live that long."

"You were right when you said the entire thing would seem crazy to me, Pepe." Raymond shook his head from side to side. "On the other hand, it does have a certain logic to it."

"I told you so."

"Yes, you did." Raymond let his breath out slowly. "I must be nuts, getting involved in something like this."

"That means you'll do it, Ramón?" Castro asked happily.

"Yes, Fidel," Raymond said. "I'll do it."

"We're all nuts!" Pepe laughed. "And I hope we all stay nuts too. It makes life interesting."

Raymond sighed, nodding.

"Tell me something, Pepe – are you really dying of cancer? You don't have to lie to me now. I'll do the surgery anyway."

"I'm dying, Ramón. I didn't lie to you about that."

"You're not scared, Pepe?"

"Of course I am. You think I'm superman? Nobody wants to die. I'm like everybody else. I don't want to die either. It's my turn, I guess."

"Are you in pain?"

"Sometimes, but it's not too bad yet. I'm told it'll get worse."

"Yes," Raymond said, averting his eyes. "It will. What symptoms do you have now?"

"Frankly, not much of anything, other than shortness of breath," Pepe said. "Like yesterday in Mexico. Do you remember when we climbed the stairs at the passport building? I got winded. That's the sort of thing that happens to me."

"Often?"

"Everytime I try to run or walk upstairs too quickly." Pepe smiled. "Otherwise, I feel okay."

Raymond said nothing. He knew from experience death was capricious. She was like a serial killer who picked who she wanted at random. She could have picked him, just as easily, instead of Pepe. The first lines of John Donne's famous poem came to his mind: 'Death Be Not Proud...'

"I'm sorry, Pepe," he said softly. "I really am."

"*Gracias, mi hermano*," Pepe said. "I appreciate your concern. As I told you, it means a lot to me."

"If I can do anything, Pepe –" Raymond's voice trailed off.

"Thank you."

"Will you be able to handle the stress of running a country such as Cuba, Pepe, plagued by so many problems? It'll make strong demands on you physically, mentally; emotionally."

"I'm used to stress, Ramón. I've lived under stress all my life."

"Yes, you have, but you've been healthy too," Raymond said. "You're not now."

"I'll manage."

"All right." Raymond looked beyond Pepe at the window behind; the breeze had died down, and the curtains were still. "Tell me the rest of the plan, Fidel. How're we going to do this car accident?"

"Teceira, *por favor*," Castro said pleasantly. "Tell Ramón the details."

CHAPTER VII

Major Teceira stood, straightened to his full length, and rearranged his uniform. Judging by his carefully manicured fingernails, neatly trimmed moustache, and well-polished shoes, Raymond suspected Teceira was a man of fastidious detail.

"We have set up a trip to Varadero for Fidel, an official visit," Teceira said in his clipped voice "He will inspect beach-front erosion and its consequence on tourism –"

"And also the decay of buildings caused by salt corrosion," Castro interrupted, smiling. "Don't forget that, Teceira. It's *very* important."

"And also the decay of buildings caused by salt corrosion," Teceira repeated, unsmiling.

"Salt corrosion?" Raymond asked.

"From the salt spray," Teceira clarified. "The *salitre* from the ocean. It oxidizes everything."

"*Salitre*," Raymond said. "I hadn't heard that word in ages."

"The accident will take place after he leaves Varadero," Teceira continued. "After he gives his main speech."

"How appropriate," Raymond said, grinning. "How will you manage to have Pepe in the car?"

"Pepe will accompany Fidel on the Varadero tour," Teceira answered smugly. "He'll pose as a Mexican expert on beach-front erosion problems and building restoration. What do you think of that, Doctor?"

"Not bad, major."

"About a mile from Varadero, on the way to Havana, there's a sharp ninety-degree curve." Teceira's forehead wrinkled as he scratched his nose. "The accident will occur there."

Teceira paused, and Raymond waited patiently for him to continue.

"The vegetation on the corner is dense, so once a car goes around the curve, it can't be seen by anyone following for a few moments."

"I see."

"Fidel will travel with only an escort trailing behind him."

"Venancio and Ramiro," Fidel explained. "The two men outside."

"Who'll be driving Fidel's car?" Raymond asked.

"He will," Teceira replied. "Sometimes he does that, so it won't be unusual."

"We've timed the curve a hundred times," Teceira said. "If Fidel takes it at around sixty miles an hour, we'll have seven to eight seconds before the escort car following behind is in sight again – plenty of time."

"I'm glad you think so." Raymond definitely didn't like Teceira's arrogant manner. "Plenty of time for what?"

"To fake the accident."

Raymond made a face, saying nothing.

"Fidel will take the car right down the middle of the curve into the vegetation," Teceira went on. "He'll drive through the trees."

Raymond raised his head to look questioningly at Fidel.

"Don't worry, Ramón." Fidel grinned. "There's no danger. I'm a pretty good driver, and I've rehearsed this accident many times before. No problem."

"But how will you fake the accident itself? I still don't understand."

"Fidel will run through a thin plywood pinned against two trees, so it makes a loud noise. Inside the car, there will be dynamite, smoke bombs and two bags filled with blood. The moment Fidel runs through the plywood, Pepe will release the smoke. As soon as the car comes to a stop, which should take less than five seconds from the time they take the curve, Pepe and Fidel will blow up the car, tear up their clothes and splash blood all over themselves. When Venancio and Ramiro arrive, they'll see only smoke, blood and a mangled car."

"Wait a moment, Teceira." Raymond raised his hand. "You're going too fast for me. How're they going to blow up the car?"

"With dynamite." Fidel laughed. "Don't worry, Ramón. Pepe and I have spent our lives blowing up things. This sort of explosion is quite easy for us. Right, Pepe?"

"Right, Fidel. Relax, Ramón. We're only blowing up the engine, not the entire car. We're just trying to make it look good."

"Absolutely." Fidel laughed loudly. "We have to look really dead when Venancio and Ramiro arrive on the scene."

"Right," Teceira said curtly. "As I said before, all they'll see is smoke, blood and a mangled car."

"Won't they check to see if Fidel is okay?"

"I'm sure they'll try. However, we'll have two things working for us there – confusion and authority."

"Confusion and authority?" Raymond repeated slowly. "Could you be more explicit, please, Teceira?"

"Of course," Teceira said in his smug manner. "Venancio and Ramiro will be confused and afraid. They won't be thinking straight."

"I agree with that," Raymond said. "Accidents are no fun. What about the authority?"

"You're looking at it, doctor." Teceira smiled and took a little bow. "I'll be the authority there."

"Where will you be, Teceira?"

"In the escort car, of course, doctor. I'll be the first to arrive at the scene of the accident. That way I'll be able to get Venancio and Ramiro out of the way and send them down the road looking for help. That's where you come in."

"Me?"

"That's right." Teceira smiled; he was obviously proud of himself and his plan. "And Ramón too. The two of you will just happen to be passing by on an ambulance on the way to the hospital, which Ramón wanted to show you while Pepe and Fidel worked in Varadero."

"Won't Venancio and Ramiro be suspicious later?" Raymond asked. "To see Ramón and me there?"

"Of what?" Teceira made a face. "Two friends visiting Varadero together who coincidentally meet on the road during an accident. There's no murder involved here or attempt against Fidel's life. It's a simple accident. Why will they suspect anything? They have no reason to."

Raymond nodded. Teceira's logic made sense to him too.

"And then what?" he asked.

"Then it'll be everything as planned. You'll transport Pepe and Fidel in the ambulance to the hospital, and we'll follow. Sonia will be there waiting. You'll perform the surgery, and that's it. Easy, don't you think?"

"Easy as pie." Raymond's voice was mocking. "You should do the surgery yourself, Teceira. You have everything else so well planned."

"I wish I could." Teceira smiled. "Unfortunately I can't. We need you for that, *Doctor*."

"Yes, you do," Raymond said. "And don't you forget it, Teceira."

The major stared at Raymond, a slight smile on his face.

"Do you want me to repeat anything, *Doctor*?"

"Yes," Raymond said. "Everything. Repeat everything again slowly, in detail, from the top. I want to make sure I understand it all."

"With pleasure," Teceira said, "*Doctor*."

Teceira's detailed explanation was everything Raymond expected – graphic, thorough and boring. When he finished, Major Teceira looked seriously into Raymond's eyes.

"Do you have any *more* questions, *Doctor*?"

Raymond had many more questions still, but he'd had enough of Teceira and his haughtiness. "None, Major."

"Then we'll leave the day after tomorrow for Varadero." He smiled triumphantly. "If that's okay with you, *Doctor*."

When Raymond awoke to go jogging at six the next morning, the sun was already up. He quickly donned his jogging shorts and tennis shoes and went out. He felt tense.

The day promised to be a scorcher, but the temperature was still bearable because of the early hour. The sky was a cloudless blue, the color of a baby's eyes. A strong humid breeze blew from the ocean.

Raymond jogged out of the hotel into the wind, heading toward the *malecón*. The wind was stronger than he expected and slowed him down. He breathed in deeply the clean penetrating air, a mixture of salt, fish and decay. He loved the odor of the sea.

Almost immediately, he started perspiring because of the humidity. He reached the *malecón* and turned left, skirting the sea wall. Waves crashed into the rocks below, creating a firework of foam. The salty spray sometimes reached him.

Several fishermen on rowboats rocked on the deep-blue waters. A ship with a flag he couldn't recognize was entering the bay. The Morro

Castle stood proudly, staring out to sea, its rocky shoulders bathed by the white foam of the crashing waves.

On the horizon, he saw the dilapidated motorboat to Regla chug across on one of its dozen daily runs. Raymond used to take the same motorboat with his father when he was a kid. Havana had not changed much in thirty years.

He overtook several joggers and numerous bikers. There was only an old blue car on the street. Crossing to the other side, Raymond headed toward the TV station building. The car followed him.

At the corner of L and 27 the traffic was heavier. He ran alongside old buses spewing dense clouds of diesel fumes, several taxis and myriad bikers. It was warmer too.

He ran back down toward the *malecón* again, where the air was cleaner and the breeze was cooler. The blue car came after him.

Raymond increased his speed, feeling self-conscious. He wondered whether he was really being followed or his fertile imagination was playing tricks on him. He turned into a side street. The blue car turned the corner behind him.

He sprinted up the street, reached the corner and turned right again, then charged toward the next corner and took another right. Once more, he headed into the strong wind and the familiar sea smells of the *malecón*. The car followed.

Raymond changed directions, jogging into a side street. He sped down the block and turned left again. The street ended in a cul de sac.

Gasping from the exertion, he retraced his steps. The old blue car turned the corner.

Raymond stopped. The car stopped too, facing him, a scant fifteen yards away. The car door opened and a man stepped out.

Raymond couldn't see him well because the sun was in his eyes. He walked up to the man, annoyed.

"What do you want?" Raymond inquired. "Why are you following me?"

"It's me, *Señor*," the man replied. "Mauricio. Remember me? I brought you from the airport yesterday."

Raymond recognized him. It was the same smiling driver who brought him from the airport the day before. He relaxed.

"Oh, yes." Raymond smiled. "You're the man who wanted shoes."

"The same."

"Did the shoes I gave you fit?"

"Very well, *Señor. Gracias*," Mauricio said. "Look! I'm wearing them now."

"If you're following me for more shoes, you're wasting your time," Raymond said. "I have no more."

"I didn't follow you for that, *Señor*," Mauricio said.

"Why did you follow me then?"

"To give you this message, *Señor*." Mauricio handed Raymond a crumpled piece of paper. "I'll come by to pick you up tonight. Have a nice day, *Señor*."

Raymond took the paper and watched, dumbfounded, as Mauricio got back in the car and drove it in reverse until he reached the top of the street. Mauricio waved from the corner and drove away in the same direction he had come.

Raymond read the note. It said:

"Things are not what they seem to be. Meet me at the club tonight at midnight. Mauricio will pick you up in front of the hotel at 11:45 p.m. sharp to take you there. Don't be late, please."

It was signed "S."

CHAPTER VIII

Raymond was finishing his breakfast at the hotel's ground floor cafeteria when Pepe appeared. Cuba seemed to agree with his friend, Raymond observed. Pepe's color was rosier than before and his eyes looked brighter.

"How was your morning jog?" Pepe inquired, plopping with a loud sigh in the chair across from Raymond. "It wasn't too hot?"

Raymond never had a chance to answer. Pepe saw a waiter nearby and his attention refocused on trying to catch the man's attention. Raymond waited patiently for the waiter finally to acknowledge Pepe.

"*Café con leche por favor!*" Pepe called out to him. "*Jugo de naranja y pan con mantequilla!*"

"Coffee with milk, orange juice, and bread with butter," Raymond repeated, smiling to his friend. "The same breakfast I had. The same breakfast we used to have as kids. Interesting, don't you think?"

"Some things never change, Ramón." Pepe groaned. "How was your jog?"

"Interesting."

Pepe gave him a curious glance, shrugged and stretched lazily. "I feel good today," he said. "I slept like a log last night."

"You look well-rested."

"And you look like shit!" Pepe broke out with loud laughter. "You look like someone who just ran five miles in the Cuban sun. Maybe jogging isn't so good for you, after all."

"Eight miles."

"That's even worse. And in this heat?"

"Some things do change, I see." Raymond smiled at his friend. "You used to be the best runner in our neighborhood when we were kids. Have you forgotten that?"

"That was a long time ago." Pepe made a face. "I'm only kidding,

Ramón. I'm jealous, I guess. You can still run, and do all those sports that I like so much, and I can't. It makes me feel – how can I say it? It makes me feel –" his voice trailed off.

"Sad?" Raymond completed his friend's sentence.

The waiter arrived with the orange juice, the bread with butter, and a steaming cup of coffee with milk. Raymond ignored him. His attention was riveted on his friend.

"Hungry!" Pepe corrected him, roaring with laughter. "Bring me more bread with butter," he told the waiter. "Lots of it. *And* scrambled eggs with ham."

"*Sí, Señor*," the waiter said.

Raymond shook his head from side to side. It was another of Pepe's jokes.

"One thing for sure," Raymond said. "You haven't lost your sense of humor... yet."

"That's the last thing I'll lose, I'll guarantee you that." Pepe drained his orange juice with one mighty swallow, gulped down half of his bread with butter and started sipping from his coffee. "Ahhhhh! How good! Anything interesting happened to you since I saw you last?"

"No," Raymond answered quickly, a little startled by his friend's question. *Was there a hidden meaning in Pepe's words?* "And to you?"

"Not a thing." Pepe guzzled his coffee the same way he guzzled his orange juice earlier. "Another coffee with milk, waiter! What do you feel like doing today, Ramón?"

"Browse around."

"Sounds good. Any specific place in mind?"

"Not really."

The waiter arrived with the bread and scrambled eggs, which he placed on the table in front of Pepe. From a nearby station, he deftly retrieved two steaming metal pots, one containing coffee and the other milk, and refilled Pepe's cup.

"*Buen provecho*," he told Pepe and left.

"*Gracias*," Pepe replied mechanically, taking a big mouthful of eggs. "Where do you want to go, Ramón? You haven't been in Cuba in thirty years. Isn't there anything you might want to do?"

"Let's take the motorboat to Regla."

"What?" Pepe stopped chewing and put his fork down. "Take the motorboat to Regla?"

"I used to take it with my father when I was a kid. I saw it this morning, going across, as I was jogging. It might be fun."

"It might be fun indeed – *la lancha de Regla*." Pepe winked at him. "I haven't done that myself in years. Actually, you won't believe this, but I was going to suggest the same thing to you."

"You're kidding."

"No, I'm not."

"Let's do it then."

"Let's do it."

"We could eat some pork with *mojo* on the other side," Raymond suggested. "They used to have the best pork in Havana on those little stands."

"All that is gone now," Pepe said sadly. "There's no food in Cuba anymore except for tourists – remember?"

"I'm sorry."

"Me too." Pepe shrugged and smiled. "I would've liked eating two or three pork sandwiches with *mojito*. Yum-Yum."

"You sure have a hearty appetite today," Raymond chided his friend. "All you talk about is food."

"Who, me?" Pepe laughed. "Waiter, can I have another orange juice?"

"How about the check too, waiter?" Raymond asked, standing. "Are we going to eat all day, Pepe, or are we going to browse?"

The docks brought back myriad forgotten memories to Raymond. The newspaper stand on the corner, facing the bay, still carried the paperback western novels he used to buy as a kid. Raymond wondered if they were the same. He leafed through a couple, and found the paper thickened with age and the pages yellowed and stained. *Could they really be the same?* he pondered.

"You remember how much we liked Max Brand when we were kids, Pepe?" Raymond showed his friend a Max Brand novel. "We thought he was the best writer in the world then."

"I still do." Pepe laughed, taking the book Raymond's from hands and riffling through it. "And I still read his novels. I have his whole collection at home."

"You're kidding."

"No."

"In English or in Spanish?"

"In both languages. I have the whole collection in English, and a few titles in Spanish from when I was a kid. He was a doctor like you, and Max Brand was his pen name. Remember?" Pepe put the book back on the shelf. "Let's catch the motorboat to Regla, Ramón. There's one about to leave."

"Let's do it."

They crossed the street and entered the ancient wooden motorboat, which was beginning to pull away slowly, almost painfully, from the dock. Several people, including two burly fishermen, rushed in behind them.

At close range, the bay waters seemed grayer than they appeared in the morning to Raymond from a distance. The engine wheezed with difficulty, spewing acrid smoke, as the peeling carcass battled the rolling waves. They sat forward, as far away from the engine as they could. There were few people on board.

"We should have our fortune told in Regla." Pepe smiled. "The best *brujo* in Cuba lives in Regla."

"My, my, how you've changed, Pepe." Raymond reproached his friend. "You were such a devout catholic when we were kids. Now you believe in fortune tellers."

Pepe shrugged, non-committal, looking out to the sea. Raymond followed his gaze. Seagulls dove playfully into the water, searching for food, and flew up again. A large school of silver sardines swam alongside the creaking boat. Pepe looked sad.

"Tell me about you, Pepe," Raymond said. "I know nothing about you."

"What do you want to know?"

"Are you married? Single? Do you have children? Where does your family live?" Raymond paused. "Tell me anything."

"I'm twice-divorced," Pepe replied. "I've two children scattered around – one in the United States and one in Brazil."

"You, the devout catholic, divorced twice?"

Pepe shrugged. "Some things do change, my friend."

"Obviously." Raymond watched silently as a seagull landed in the bay waters with a splash and flew up again a moment later happily carrying a wriggling sardine in his beak. "What are they? Your children, I mean. Boys? Girls?"

"Two boys – two men, really – one from each marriage. The older is twenty-eight; the younger ten."

"Do you see them often?"

"Not as often as I'd like. One is now in Okinawa with the marines. The other lives in Rio de Janeiro with his mother who doesn't let him see me."

"Why not?"

"Who knows?" Pepe shrugged. "You know how women are. You spend twenty years married to a woman you think you know, divorce her, and suddenly realize you were married to a total stranger. You know what I mean?"

"No," Raymond answered. "I was married twenty-two years to the same woman till she died. I don't know what you mean."

"Well, you feel like shit, my friend. You lose confidence. You lose your faith in humanity. You become confused."

"I see."

Pepe turned to his friend and fixed him with a stare. "Do you?"

"Not really."

Pepe looked away again.

"We're almost on the other side," Raymond said. Pepe didn't answer. He was immersed in his thoughts.

"It looks different from what I remember," Raymond said. "Kind of empty. There are no shops anymore."

"I told you so." Pepe smiled sadly at his friend. "To me it looks desolate."

"Desolate is a good word." Raymond watched Pepe with curiosity. "You're back from your deep thoughts, I see."

"I'm back. Life's too short to spend it brooding – particularly mine."

Raymond said nothing. He watched the motorboat approach the dock carefully. The pilot threw a rope to an old man with a sailor hat who swiftly tied it to a peeling wooden post. The motorboat stopped, and they got up to leave.

"Did you notice the two men who came on the boat behind us, Pepe?" Raymond asked.

"I did."

Walking the streets of Regla, Raymond realized he had forgotten much about his past. He couldn't remember any of the streets. Pepe seemed to know where he was going, though. He navigated around the narrow cobble stoned streets like a man with a purpose.

They roamed around the old fishing village, entering at random empty fishing shops impregnated with the smell of the sea.

The streets bustled with activity and loud conversation. Pepe stopped in front of an old white house surrounded by a wrought-iron fence; the house needed paint. He rang the doorbell.

A creaking door opened and an old wrinkled woman peeked out.

"What do you want?" she asked.

"Is Juan, the *brujo*, in?" Pepe asked.

"No," she replied curtly.

"Where is he?" Pepe insisted. "We came to have our fortunes told."

"He's gone."

"Where to?" Pepe asked. "We'd like to find him."

"He's racing his horse," the woman explained. "Nube."

"Where?"

The old woman made a vague motion with her arm, pointing down the road. "Over there. By the railroad tracks."

"*Gracias*," Pepe said.

The woman slammed the door shut.

"I guess we won't have our fortunes told today," Pepe said amiably. "It's a shame. He's a good *brujo*."

"Maybe we can find another one," Raymond suggested.

"No, this is the good one." Pepe started marching down the street. "Come, Ramón. Let's go to the horse races. Did you know they have lots of street horse races in Regla? You ever have been to one?"

"No."

"I'll take you to one today."

They marched down the street away from the village. They crossed an old railroad track and turned into an open field full of *campesinos* that had congregated, apparently, to watch a horse race. Two horses with their riders were in the middle of the crowd. Raymond and Pepe mixed with the group. After a while the two fishermen from the motorboat arrived and mixed with the group too.

"Which horse do you like?" Pepe asked Raymond, approaching the horses. "You have a favorite?"

Raymond didn't know much about horses. He inspected them with curiosity. One was a young and nervous pinto; the other was an old white horse.

"The pinto, I guess," Raymond replied. "He seems younger and more powerful. The other is an old horse."

"True," Pepe agreed. "But what an old horse!"

"Which one do you like?"

"Always bet on experience." Pepe laughed. "The white horse will win."

"You seem very sure."

"Watch."

The riders lined up their horses at the top of the dusty road for the start. The riders matched the horses. The man riding the pinto was young and powerful; the rider of the white horse was an old wizened *campesino* with remarkable blue eyes, which contrasted sharply with his dark, sun-rugged features.

One of the *campesinos* gave the start, and the horses sprinted neck and neck in a cloud of dust toward a finish line marked by two dying trees. The motley crowd of onlookers who had gathered to watch the race shouted and whistled their encouragement. Almost at the end, the white horse pulled in front of the pinto and crossed the finish line a nose ahead.

"See?" Pepe smiled at Raymond.

"How did you know?"

"Come and I'll tell you," Pepe said. "Let's see the winning horse."

They cut a path through the *campesinos* until they reached the sweating white horse and his beaming rider. There was a commotion caused by the rider of the pinto horse as he whipped his horse in anger. Two *campesinos* took his whip away and quieted him down.

Pepe patted the white horse's chest.

"Raymond," he said, smiling. "This here is Juan Contreras, the best *brujo* in Regla. Don't shake hands or look up. Remember we're being followed. Pat the horse and smile."

Raymond patted the horse and smiled. He felt dumb.

"If something were to happen to me, Juan will be your contact. He can help you with anything. Even get you out of Cuba, if necessary." Pepe spoke rapidly, hardly moving his lips. "Clandestine boats leave Regla at night for the US. Juan can get you on one of those. He knows the people who do it. Come to his house, and he'll take it from there. You know where he lives."

"The house where we stopped on the way over, and the old woman came out?"

"That's right. Number nineteen Guevara Street. Can you remember that?"

Raymond nodded.

"I'll give you his telephone later. Please, don't mention Juan to anyone," Pepe said. "Not even to Sonia. *Comprendes?*"

"*Sí.*"

"It's for your own good."

Raymond nodded again.

"Nice horse," Pepe said loudly, patting the horse first and then shaking hands with the rider. "Congratulations."

Raymond was so fidgety, he went downstairs at 10 p.m. He browsed around the sparse shops, drank a *mojito* at Las Canitas, and paced restlessly up and down the threadbare carpet on the lobby. His mind was filled with speculation.

Raymond was alone. Castro had sent a car earlier to collect Pepe and drive him to Varadero where they were to meet. Teceira called shortly afterwards to tell Raymond that Sonia and Mon would pick him up next morning at the scheduled time. They would all meet at a Varadero hotel.

"I need amplified front and side face pictures of Fidel and Pepe for the operation," Raymond told Teceira. "I need them at the operating room."

"Why didn't you say so before, doctor?"

"I thought you knew. You seem to know everything else."

There was a long silence before Teceira replied.

"You'll have them," he said. "You want color or black-and-white?

"Color, if possible."

"All right." Teceira's voice was curt. "Be ready on time tomorrow, doctor. Every minute counts on this mission."

Since I arrived in Cuba everybody tells me to be on time, Raymond thought as he hung up. *Incredible.*

At eleven, Raymond was desperate. He crossed the street to the well-lighted Copelia ice-cream shop on the ground floor of the *Instituto Cubano de Radio y Televisión,* once known as the CMQ Television Station. The shop was adjacent to the Cine Yara, which Raymond remembered from his childhood days as the finest cinema in Havana, although, much as he tried, he couldn't recollect its old name.

Copelia was full of smiling people, mostly tourists, chatting animatedly. He ordered a *mamey* ice, which immediately brought to his mind memories of the Chinese ice cream shop in his old neighborhood he frequented with his mother as a child.

Mauricio was on time. As Raymond started to cross the street back to the Havana Libre, the blue car pulled up by the curb, and the front passenger door opened.

"*Entre rápido, Doctor,*" Mauricio said, looking over his shoulders to see if they were being watched. "Come in, quickly!"

Raymond got in the car and closed the door. The ancient sedan barreled down the street, the once-powerful V-8 engine coughing and sputtering at full blast, the once-sleek body squeaking loudly at every bump on the road.

"Are we being followed?" Raymond asked. "Is someone behind us?"

Mauricio inspected carefully the rearview mirror. "I don't think so."

"Why the rush then?"

"One can't be too careful, *Doctor.*"

The Profesionales Club buried Raymond in an unexpected avalanche of mixed emotions. Dilapidated and unkempt, the club was a distant sad memory of its old gay self. According to Mauricio, it was being used both as a neighborhood recreation center and party office building. A single light shone from a square window on the ground floor of the darkened surroundings.

Mauricio pointed to the light.

"Sonia's expecting you," he said. "That's her office."

Raymond got out of the car, and Mauricio started to drive away.

"Wait!" Raymond called. "Where are you going?"

Mauricio stopped the car with a screeching of brakes. "Home."

"How do I get back to the hotel?"

"Sonia will take you."

"Oh."

"*Adiós, Doctor.*"

The car drove away. Raymond heard it squeaking in the dark for a long time. Finally, he turned and walked on the cement steps toward Sonia's office.

CHAPTER IX

The moonless night was balmy and full of stars. Closed and dark, the ballroom where he once danced his graduation waltz with Sonia had a big sign on the front door: *Administración*. Raymond peeked in through one of the windows. The dance area had been converted to offices.

A light wind rustled the trees, filling his nostrils with a familiar scent from his youth he identified with the period of time he dated Sonia. It was a mixture of jasmine, night air, sea breeze, and the slightly pungent smell of his adrenalin. It was the smell of anticipation.

Taking a deep breath, he entered the building. He found Sonia in her office, sitting behind an imposing desk cluttered with mountains of paper. She smiled and came from behind her desk to greet him. She wore a sleeveless white cotton dress with her hair pulled back.

Raymond realized how beautiful she was still. His heart pounded as furiously as when he was an amorous teenager in the throes of passion, arriving at Sonia's house to take her out on a date under the supervision of her vigilant mother. He didn't know whether to kiss her or not, so he did nothing. He simply stood awkwardly in front of her, much like a teenager would. He felt strangely shy and vulnerable.

So did Sonia, it seemed. For once, she appeared self-conscious, uncertain as to what to do next. A cricket sang outside once. Raymond was aware of how alone they were in the empty surroundings.

"So," he said. "How are you, Sonia?"

"Fine." Her smile widened. "And you, Ramón?"

"*Muy bien, gracias.*"

"I'm glad you could make it. There're some things we should discuss."

"So I gathered by your note."

"You want something to drink, Ramón? Coffee?"

He shook his head no. "You always work this late, Sonia?"

"Sometimes." She made a face. "Not usually, though."

He looked around the office. It was sparsely decorated, except for plants and numerous photographs in picture frames of different sizes scattered around her desk and credenza tops. Raymond picked one of them at random. A small child with light hair, a big smile and sad eyes stared at him.

"Mon?" he asked. She nodded.

Raymond felt the sharp pain of guilt. There were easily two-dozen pictures, chronicling Mon's life from birth to present day, including a large eight-by-ten glossy of his medical school graduation.

There was a picture of Mon in uniform too. Raymond inspected it with curiosity. Ramón displayed the same boyish smile he had as a child – and the same sad eyes.

"I didn't realize Mon was in the army," Raymond remarked.

"Air Force." Sonia corrected him. "A captain *and* a pilot."

"I'm impressed."

"You should be," Sonia said. "He used to fly Mig-29s. He's no longer active in the Air Force, though. He hasn't flown in nearly two years. Taking care of Fidel is a full-time occupation."

"Are the pictures in chronological order, Sonia?"

"More or less."

"Where do they begin?"

"At the credenza."

He picked up what he thought could be the first picture. It was a large black-and-white photograph in an ornate silver frame. A young couple in evening clothes smiled at the camera. She was blonde and beautiful in her long formal gown; he was handsome and elegant in his tuxedo. They were Sonia and he.

"Your graduation dance picture," she explained. "Do you remember your graduation dance?"

"Of course."

"It was right here."

"I know," he said.

"Since you've forgotten other things, I thought you could have forgotten that too."

He didn't answer her. There was a reproachful tone in her voice he didn't like.

"How long have you been working here, Sonia?" he asked.

"Four years and two months."

"Is it hard?"

"The work?"

"No, not the work itself. Is it hard to work here in the same place where..."

"Where what?" Sonia asked. "Where we had your graduation dance?"

"No, not that," he replied. "Where we..."

"Where we made love for the first time?" she completed his sentence, and he felt embarrassed. "Is that what you want to say?"

"Yes," he answered flatly. "That's what I want to say."

"No." She looked him straight in the eye. "It isn't hard."

He raised an inquiring eyebrow at her, saying nothing.

"In fact, I *asked* for the job," she said.

"I beg your pardon?"

"I asked for the job," she repeated. "When the old director left, I applied for the opening and got it."

Raymond edged closer to Sonia. Her green eyes were brighter and more beautiful than ever.

"Doesn't it bring you memories from your youth, Sonia?" he asked softly.

"We grow up and forget," she replied, a sad smile on her face. "We learn quickly as adults how to conjugate the verb forget – I forget, you forget, we forget." She stopped. "You forgot too, Ramón, didn't you?"

He lowered his head for a moment, and then raised it again.

"Maybe I did," he answered. "And I'm sorry for that. But it's all coming back to me fast since I returned to Havana. I feel as confused and as much in love now as I was when I was eighteen."

He held her hand. It was cold. She shook her hand off.

"Why did you leave me, Ramón?"

"I didn't mean to leave you, Sonia. All I wanted to do was go away for a while and get my degree. You *know* that." He looked out the window into the darkness outside, seeing nothing. "I didn't realize it was going to turn out like this. I thought I was going to see you again soon. Things changed very quickly in the United States. Remember, I was only—"

"Eighteen," she said. "I know how old you were. I was eighteen too."

"Yes."

"Why didn't you answer my letters, Ramoncito?"

"I did, at first," Raymond replied. "With time each of your letters became more difficult to answer, Sonia. I was caught between two worlds. I was squeezed between two different cultures. You can't understand how difficult it was for me."

"I'm trying to understand, Ramón."

"My whole world changed, Sonia. When I left Cuba, it was like a game. I felt like I was going away for a short trip, and I was coming back soon. Living in the United States was no game, though. Getting into medical school was tough. Staying in was even tougher. I spent longer and longer hours studying. I had no time for anything, Sonia."

"You can write a letter in five minutes, Ramón. It doesn't take a long time."

"The Castro situation didn't help either. I identified more and more with the United States and less and less with Cuba. I guess, to put it another way, I stopped being a Cuban so I could become an American."

"That's why you didn't write? It doesn't make any sense to me."

"It's hard to explain. I was split down the middle. The only way I could survive was to eliminate from my mind all things Cuban. I had too many other things I was dealing with – school, a new country, a new language, a new life."

"So you eliminated me."

"I didn't mean to."

"But you did."

"Yes." He sighed. "I did."

She leaned on her desk, looking behind his back somewhere into space. She looked forlorn and dejected. He wished so much to hold her in his arms to console her, but he didn't dare to. He was afraid how Sonia would react.

"Well," she said suddenly. "The facts of life. I just learned the facts of life again. I thought I knew them all already, but I guess I didn't. Come, Ramón, let me show you the grounds."

She rose to her full length, a determined expression on her face. She walked toward the door.

"Did you really forget me, Sonia?" he asked her.

She stopped and turned around.

"I wish I had, Raymond. I wish I had."

They strolled around the garden following the cemented walkway, which meandered around rose and jasmine trees and thick bushes. The stars were so bright they saw each other clearly, even though there were no lights outside. Sonia stepped off the walkway and paced on the thick lawn until she reached a covered place under the trees where they were surrounded by jasmine bushes and hedges. She faced Raymond.

"You know where you are, Ramón?" she asked.

The area seemed vaguely familiar to Raymond. The fragrance of jasmine enveloped him.

"Is it–" He stopped.

"Yes," Sonia answered the unfinished question. "This is the place where we made love for the first time."

He didn't know what to say, so he said nothing.

Sonia moved closer to him. He felt her body heat. She looked him in the eye.

"Make love to me," she said. "I've waited thirty years for this moment."

His heart tried to hammer its way out of his ribcage. The nape of his neck was aflame. *My blood pressure must be a thousand,* he thought fleetingly. Then Sonia's lips were warm and moist; and her tongue was probing and daring at the same time.

He closed his eyes and responded to her kiss hungrily, letting himself go. He felt the hardened tips of her breasts pressing against his chest, and the incredible heat generated by his own loins and hers.

They were teenagers again, crazy with unrestrained passion and untried love. They wrenched their clothes off their bodies and fell to the ground intertwined in a desperate embrace. An exquisite myriad of fireworks exploded in Raymond's head. As they coupled, fused into one, he released his entire being to an overwhelmingly powerful and passionate intensity he had long forgotten…

Raymond looked up at the stars, feeling spent and satisfied. He and Sonia lay on the lawn, naked; their crumpled and torn clothes rested a few steps away.

"There's no one here at the club?" Raymond asked.

"No one."

He looked at the heap of crumpled clothes.

"Our clothes are going to be wrinkled." He laughed.

"Let them." Sonia smiled. "I've coveted this moment for thirty years. Who cares about clothes right now?"

"Was this moment what you thought it would be, Sonia?"

She looked at him. He could see the brightness of her eyes in the darkness. "Better," she replied. "Definitely better than the first time we made love. And for you?"

"I didn't think it was possible to feel so young and in love again." He leaned forward and kissed her. "Thank you, Sonia."

"For what?"

"For being you."

"You're welcome."

He was silent and reflective for a while.

"I thought you told me you were happy with Teceira, Sonia," Raymond said quietly.

"I said I was satisfied."

"Are you?"

She looked at him and smiled. "Not anymore."

Raymond remained silent.

"It's been awful, Ramón," Sonia said after a while. "You don't know what I've suffered all these years, going to bed with one man while desiring another. I would close my eyes when Humberto made love to me and imagined he was you."

Raymond felt a pang of jealousy as he projected the scene in his mind. He stared at the stars again. They flickered brightly in the night.

"But he's a good man, isn't he?" he said.

"Sometimes."

He looked at her. "Sometimes?"

"Sometimes he's a pompous ass, mean and despicable."

"Mon loves him very much, doesn't he?" Raymond was bewildered. "At least, he seems to."

"He does. Humberto is different with Mon. He loves Mon as if he were his own son."

"That's not bad."

"No," Sonia agreed. "But he loves and hates me. He loves me because he can't help himself. He hates me because he knows I've always loved you. And he hates you!"

"He seems fine with me, isn't he?"

"No," she said flatly. "That's another reason I asked you to come here tonight."

"What do you mean?"

"I'm afraid, Ramoncito."

"Afraid of what, Sonia?"

"Afraid for you – for Mon, for me, for all of us. This operation gives me the creeps. There's something very wrong in all this. I just don't know what it is."

"Are you guessing, Sonia – or do you have something specific in mind?"

"You can call it a woman's intuition." She looked at him and saw the expression on his face. "Oh, I forgot. You're a scientist, a doctor. You want hard facts."

"Yes." He nodded. "You have any?"

"No. It's a lot of different things, Ramón. I just don't know how to explain it to you. Conversations overhead on the phone between Humberto and Pepe and Fidel, a certain attitude, a way of saying things." Sonia let out a deep breath. "I've been married to the man for thirty years. I know him well."

"What are you trying to tell me, Sonia?"

"If you perform the surgery, they'll probably kill you – and maybe Mon and me too."

He sat up. "Why do you say that, Sonia?"

"Can't you see it, Ramón?" she asked him. "We'd be the only witnesses. They'll have to kill us."

"Pepe wouldn't allow that, Sonia," Raymond said. "He would

protect us."

"I don't know if he would, or could, Ramón."

"What do you mean by that, Sonia?"

"God knows I love Pepe very much. He's been a true friend all my life – sometimes my only friend. But I don't know, Ramoncito. Sometimes I think he's really an undercover agent for the Castro government. He comes and goes as he pleases in Cuba. And he and Fidel are very close friends. What kind of CIA agent can he be, Ramón? Think about it."

"What are you really saying, Sonia?"

"I believe I said it already, Ramón. Pepe might be really a Castro agent planted in the United States."

"And he might not be, Sonia. He could also be a CIA agent planted in Cuba."

"Or both."

"Both?"

"A double agent, Ramón."

"Even if he is, Sonia, and I hope he isn't, what does that have to do with us? With this operation?"

"Sometimes you can be so naive, Ramón. Maybe that's why I love you so much," Sonia said. "Pepe's the one who planned this whole operation with Fidel and Humberto, right? Cuban Intelligence doesn't like to leave loose ends, that much I know. And neither does the CIA. Mon, you and I would be loose ends. Now you understand why I'm afraid?"

Raymond turned Sonia's words over in his mind carefully.

"There's nothing we can do now," he said. "We're trapped in this operation. For the time being, all we can do is watch closely how things develop – and hope you're wrong about Pepe."

Sonia's warm hand touched his chest, sending a shiver throughout his body.

"There's something you can do now."

"What?"

"You can make love to me again."

CHAPTER X

On Friday after lunch, Raymond left for Varadero accompanied by Sonia and Mon. Mauricio drove the car. It was the same squeaking clunker Raymond knew so well.

Pepe and Teceira were to meet them at the hotel for dinner to go over the plan one last time. The accident was scheduled to take place on Sunday after Castro's big speech.

The three of them were silent and thoughtful, immersed in their own worlds. Raymond tried to go over in his mind the salient points of the disturbing conversation he'd had with Sonia the night before, but all he could think about was the feeling of her body as they made love. Sonia looked radiant.

"A penny for your thoughts," Sonia said to him.

"Radiocentro," Raymond said.

"I beg your pardon?"

"Radiocentro," Raymond repeated, smiling broadly. "For the last two days, I've been racking my brains trying to remember the name of the Yara cinema thirty years ago, and I simply couldn't. It's Radiocentro, isn't it?"

"It is. Why didn't you ask me? I could've told you."

"I wanted to remember it all by myself."

"Well, you did"

"Yes, I did." He shook his head in disbelief. "It's amazing how things are coming back to me now. At first, I couldn't remember *anything*."

"And now?"

"It's a strange feeling, Sonia." He chuckled. "I'm thoroughly confused. It's as if I've gone back in time to when I lived in Cuba. My mind's all jumbled-up."

"Jumbled-up? What do you mean?"

"It's as if my mind is trying to erase all my American memory tapes, and is playing only the old Cuban tapes from my youth." He frowned with puzzlement. "I feel like a kid again."

"You're doing extremely well for a kid." Sonia squeezed his hand, a picaresque grin on her face. "Remembering, I mean."

They sat in the back seat of the car. Mon sat up front with Mauricio, neither seemingly paying attention to their conversation.

Raymond watched his son's hair blowing in the wind. The afternoon was sweltering hot, in spite of the breeze streaming through the car's open windows.

He had forgotten how breathtakingly beautiful the Cuban landscape was. Mile after mile, they passed lush, tropical-green countryside laced with royal palm trees and interspersed with quaint little villages.

"*Cubita la bella*," Sonia said. "Didn't you miss her?"

"Not until now," Raymond replied.

"*Papá* called this morning," Mon said abruptly, turning to face Raymond. "He'll have the pictures you requested for you to see this evening at dinner. He told me to tell you. Is that all right, or would you prefer to see them earlier? He said he could have them delivered to the hotel this, afternoon, if you wanted. He's not staying at the hotel with us, and neither is Pepe."

Raymond was astonished. "They're not?"

"No."

"Why not?"

"I think they have some last-minute planning to do before the accident," Mon said. "They're staying with Fidel tonight to go over things once more. Fidel is very detailed, and *Papá* is even worse."

Sonia and Raymond exchanged a quick, questioning glance. She shrugged almost imperceptibly.

"Tonight is fine," Raymond told Mon. "Don't forget also we need to give Pepe and Fidel a physical before the surgery. I don't want any surprises on the operating table."

"Right." Mon's voice was clipped, just like Teceira's. "It's scheduled for four o'clock tomorrow afternoon."

He turned his head and looked forward again. Raymond stared at the unfamiliar nape of his son's neck. It felt weird to have a son he didn't know.

"You don't like me much, do you, Mon?" Raymond spoke to his son's back. "Would you mind telling me why?"

"Again?" Mon turned around to look at him, a mortified expression on his face. "I thought I'd told you already the other day. What else is there to say, doctor?"

"Doctor?"

"Aren't you a doctor?"

"I'm also your father."

"You want me to call you father?"

"No, I want you to tell me why you hate me so much," Raymond replied amiably, trying not to lose his temper. "Last time you told me you did. Now I'd like to know why."

"Right now is not the time or the place," Mon said. "Besides, we're arriving in Varadero. We'll be at the hotel in ten minutes

"We have ten minutes

"Let's wait till later when we can be alone." Mon gave his mother a worried look. "Some things are better not discussed in public.'‘

"Your mother is hardly the public."

"I don't want to discuss this in front of her or Mauricio."

"When then?"

"How about tomorrow night? We could get together for dinner, if you want, and discuss the subject at length."

"Why not tonight after dinner?" Raymond suggested. "We could have a drink and talk."

"I can't tonight." Mon smiled his boyish smile. "I have a previous engagement with a lovely young girl I've been seeing in Varadero – if you don't mind."

"I don't mind." Raymond shrugged. "I've waited this long, I can wait another day. Tomorrow night it is."

Seeing Varadero beach after thirty years made Raymond emotional. Childhood memories stirred inside him again with painful intensity.

They were staying at a small four-story wooden hotel on the beach Ramón knew, which accepted Cubans – something that seemed more rare every day. Foreigners and their dollars were accepted everywhere; Cubans, surprisingly, were not.

"Tourism apartheid," Sonia called it. "But necessary for the economy."

"I thought socialism was supposed to be for the people," Raymond commented. "Not for the economy."

"Without some form of economy, there'll be no people," Sonia said. "A poor country demands sacrifice of its citizens."

"So did the catholic church during the dark ages, Sonia."

"The catholic church in the dark ages was built on ignorance and lies," Sonia said sharply. "Our system is built on truth."

Raymond shook his head, not believing what he heard. Sonia was, it seemed, a committed revolutionary.

"Say whatever you want," Raymond said. "It's not right."

They checked in at the hotel, which was owned by two old American sisters who forfeited their nationality during the sixties and remained in Cuba during the revolution. Named Rosa and Maria, they both had false teeth, dyed red hair, large sagging breasts, and wrinkled, heavily powdered faces. They inquired about Major Teceira, giggling like schoolgirls, and were delighted to learn he was coming for dinner.

Teceira arrived punctually, dressed in a freshly ironed uniform. Raymond realized he hated the man. It wasn't so much what Teceira did or didn't do. He was simply jealous.

"Here are the pictures," Teceira said, handing Raymond a large manila envelope. "Are they all right?"

Teceira had done his job well. There were easily two-dozen full-blown photographs of both Fidel and Pepe.

"Where's Pepe?" Raymond asked.

"With Fidel. He couldn't come."

"What do you think?" Raymond showed Mon the pictures.

"I'm not a plastic surgeon. That's why you're here."

"What do you think, anyway?"

"Fidel has bags under his eyes and a slightly bigger nose than Pepe's," Mon replied thoughtfully. "Also a bigger chin."

"That's right," Raymond said. "You're pretty observant. You would've made a good plastic surgeon. It's actually easier to convert Fidel to Pepe than Pepe to Fidel."

"So what do we do?"

"We can do several things, providing we have the equipment," Raymond replied. "If we don't have the equipment, we *are* in trouble."

"What do you need?"

"I need equipment to do liposuction on Pepe. I need to extract some fat from his waist to put bags under his eyes. I also need a prosthesis, so I can implant a bigger chin."

"We have both. I told you medicine in Cuba is more advanced than you think it is."

"I'd like to see your equipment anyway," Raymond said. "I don't like to take things for granted. For the moment, I'll take your word for it."

"What else do you need?" Mon's voice was curt.

"Nothing much. I can make Pepe's nose bigger by taking cartilage out of his ear and putting it in his nose, so that's no problem. The hair we'll handle with a wig, although I would've preferred doing a transplant. I think we're okay. All we need to do now is check both of them and have blood tests done."

"We're scheduled to do both tomorrow afternoon. Is that early enough?"

"That's fine," Raymond said.

As soon as dinner was over, Mon checked his watch, said he was in a hurry and departed. Teceira excused himself, saying he was late for his meeting with Fidel and Pepe, and left too. Mauricio mumbled he had something to do and disappeared. To his surprise, Sonia complained of having a headache and vanished too.

"*C'est la vie,*" Raymond said to himself.

He was in bed and asleep by ten.

The click of the turning doorknob awoke him in the middle of the night. At first, Raymond thought someone was breaking into his bedroom. He listened to the door opening softly, and he got ready to jump on the intruder. Then he smelled the perfume and knew it was Sonia.

He remained motionless as she padded daintily on the threadbare carpet, removed her robe and climbed in his bed. Her skin felt silky and hot as she pressed her body against his. She was naked.

"I couldn't sleep, Ramoncito," she said. "I know you're awake. Make love to me."

A fire truck bell clanged loudly. The truck rushed toward Raymond. He knew he had to get out of the way, but he couldn't. He opened his eyes. It was the telephone. He checked his watch. The phosphorescent dial told him it was two in the morning.

He groped for the receiver in the dark, wondering who would be calling him at such an hour and why.

"*Bueno?*"

He recognized the voice immediately. It was Teceira.

"Do you know where Sonia is?" he asked.

Sonia slept soundly by his side. He ran his fingers up her spine, and she purred like a contented kitten.

"No," Raymond lied. "Why?"

"I've been calling her room, and she doesn't answer."

"Maybe her phone is broken," Raymond suggested. "Everything else seems to be broken in Cuba. Maybe her phone is too."

"Maybe."

"What do you want, Teceira? I hope you didn't call me in the middle of the night to ask me about Sonia?"

"No."

"Why did you call me then?"

"The accident has been moved forward one day. It'll take place tomorrow morning instead of Sunday as we planned."

"Why?" He sat up in bed, alarmed. "What's wrong?"

"Raul Castro is coming back from Russia, we just learned. His talks didn't go as well as expected, so he aborted his trip and is returning home. He'll be in Havana Sunday. We need to stage the accident and perform the surgery before he arrives – and that only leaves tomorrow."

"But we're not ready yet."

"We'll have to be. It's got to be tomorrow. The accident will take place at ten. Mon will pick you up at nine in the ambulance. Be ready."

"Have you talked to Mon already?"

"Yes."

"I haven't checked the equipment, Teceira."

"Mon has."

"But I haven't. And I'm the one doing the surgery."

Teceira wasn't listening.

"Tell Sonia too, when you see her. Please."

"We haven't examined Fidel and Pepe either, Teceira. We need to do that before –"

He was talking to a dead line.

BOOK
TWO

CHAPTER XI

The hard rain that rattled the windowpanes woke Raymond at daybreak. Sonia was gone. He got out of bed to peek outside.

It was a wet morning. The rain came down in thick sheets; the sea was slate-gray and turbulent; the beach was deserted. He decided to skip jogging for one day.

Mon knocked on his door shortly after eight. He looked relaxed and freshly-shaven.

"Came by early so I could take you to check out the equipment, as you wanted," he said to Raymond. "You feel like breakfast?"

"Never eat before surgery," Raymond replied. "But I'll have coffee with you."

The two sisters were up already. They were bundled-up with bulky sweaters.

"Awful day," Rosa said.

"And chilly," Maria added.

Raymond and Mon had coffee and left. The violent rain had turned into a pestering drizzle. The temperature had dropped ten degrees easily because of the thunderstorm, but it was hardly cold.

"The sisters have been in Cuba so long, they feel cold if the weather changes," Mon chuckled. "They're like my twin grandmothers. I've known them for years."

"Where's your mother?" Raymond asked. "Isn't she coming with us?"

"Mauricio picked her up already. She's at the hospital getting things ready for us."

The ambulance was parked on the street in front of the hotel. White with red letters, it wasn't quite as old as Mauricio's dinosaur but not by much. The engine coughed and sputtered.

"All we need now is for this ambulance not to start," Raymond said.

"That would be something."

"Don't worry. *Papá* had it thoroughly checked yesterday. It always does this in the morning."

The engine cranked up, at last. Mon revved the big V-8 for a couple of minutes to warm it up. He pulled away from the curb, steering the bulky vehicle down the wet street. Raymond noticed two big improvements over Mauricio's car – the ambulance was automatic, and it didn't squeak.

The hospital was in a clearing in the woods reachable by a winding asphalt road. It was a white square prefabricated construction without windows with a single entrance door and a corrugated zinc roof. A locked gate barred access. A sign announced that the hospital was closed all week due to remodeling and directed patients to another unit nearby.

Mon tooted the horn three times, and Mauricio ran out of the building. He unlocked the gate for them.

"Your mother's waiting for you inside," he told Mon. "How're you feeling today?"

"Great," Mon answered. "And you?"

"Nervous." He grinned at Raymond. "And you, *Doctor?*"

"Nervous too."

Mon parked the ambulance in front of the front door, and they went inside. They found Sonia in front of the surgery room.

"I thought you weren't coming, Mon," Sonia said, nervously "It's after nine already. You don't have much time left."

"Enough," Mon said. "We're only two minutes away from where the accident will take place."

Sonia looked ravishing to Raymond in her nurse's clothes and without make-up. Her skin was rosy and devoid of wrinkles. Raymond decided lovemaking was excellent for her complexion.

"Whatever you say." Sonia smiled at Raymond. "Let me show you around. Mon has seen this place already."

Mon appeared hesitant for a moment, as if a hidden message had been transmitted to him by her mother's words. He looked from one to the other.

"I'll wait outside," he said to Raymond. "Hurry up. We've got to leave in ten minutes."

He marched out. Raymond watched him thoughtfully.

"Was there a special communication between you?" he asked Sonia. "Or did I just imagine it?"

"He's my son," she answered, pushing the swinging-doors to the surgery room. "We understand each other. We tell each other everything. He tells me everything, and I tell him everything."

"What does that mean?" Raymond asked suspiciously.

"He knows about us."

"Oh, my God!" Raymond halted. "How? Did you tell him?"

"I had to. He saw me coming out of your room this morning."

"I thought he looked at me funny when he came to get me." Raymond was pensive. "How did he react?"

"Hurt, at first. He seemed to understand better later. We had a long talk."

"What is he going to do?"

"Nothing. He'll probably talk to you about it, though."

Raymond sighed. He shook his head from side to side.

"Show me the surgery room," he said. "This problem will have to wait. We have a complicated surgery to do first."

"First you have to kiss me," she said, hugging him tightly. Her eyes were bright green, like a cat's. "Then, you can do everything else."

"The best proposition I've had since I've been in Cuba," he said, kissing her. Her lips were soft and supple, her body warm. "What else do you have in mind?"

"To show you the surgery room." She broke the embrace and pushed him away. "We don't have much time for anything else."

The surgery room was larger than he expected, and well stocked with supplies.

"I tried to bring everything I thought you might need," Sonia said. "Mon helped me."

"What do you have?"

"What do you need?"

"Non-traumatic needles, two-zero and four-zero stitches for the lift and the eyes–"

"Silk or Dexon?" Sonia interrupted him.

"Either one will do," Raymond replied. "I prefer Dexon, if you have it."

"I have it, *Doctor*." She smiled. "I also have silk. What else do you need?"

"Blades twelve and fifteen, catgut for under the skin, scalpels – of course."

"We've got them all," Sonia said. "We also have an aspirator to do the liposuction and two-and-three-millimeter canules."

"I don't need them anymore. I changed my mind."

"You're not going to do the liposuction anymore?"

"No," he replied. "I'm going to take fat out of the belly surgically and implant it under Pepe's eyes. I think there will be less possibility of complications later. Where are the photographs? I need to see them."

Sonia opened a set of curtains and showed Raymond two operating tables side by side. The walls beyond the tables were covered with full-blown color photographs of Pepe and Fidel in all possible positions.

"Do you think we have enough pictures, *Doctor*?"

"I think you have enough of everything," he answered. "You have anesthetic too?"

"All you want."

"I believe it." He laughed. "Let's go bring the patients in, so we can get started."

He turned to leave, and she held his arm.

"Good luck, Ramoncito." She kissed him lightly on the lips. "Take care of yourself and Mon. I love you both."

The road was lightly transited. They saw three bikers, one truck and two buses, but not a car.

"One more turn of the road, and we'll be there," Mon said. "Time to synchronize our watches. We'll stop under those trees ahead and wait. We still have time."

"You seem to know this area well."

"I was assigned to Varadero with the Air Force," Mon said. "The base is less than a mile from here hidden in the bushes."

"You're a pilot, I hear."

"That's right."

90

"What do you fly?"

"Mig twenty-nines mostly."

"You like flying?"

"I love it, but I love medicine more."

"Amazing," Raymond said, grinning. "Simply amazing."

"What?"

"I wanted to be a pilot when I was a kid. Obviously, I loved medicine more too."

Mon brought the vehicle to a stop. "What time do you have?" he asked.

"Nine fifty-one."

"I have nine fifty-two," he said. "Let's synchronize our watches at nine fifty-two, all right?"

"All right."

"We'll stay here till nine fifty-seven. Then we'll move."

Raymond nodded.

"One more thing," Mon said curtly. "I know about you and mother, and I don't like it. As far as I'm concerned, you've been nothing but trouble since you arrived. *Papá* would kill you if he knew. I won't say anything to him on one condition."

"What's that?"

"You finish the surgery, and you leave – and you never come back to Cuba again."

"I see." Raymond raised an eyebrow. "And if I don't?"

Mon looked at Raymond with steady eyes. He pursed his lips.

"If you don't, doctor," he said. "I'll tell *Papá*, who'll kill you on the spot – that is, if I don't kill you myself."

"I'm your father, Mon. Will you kill your own father?"

"You're not my father, I already told you!" Ramón barked. "You're a biological accident. My father is Humberto Teceira, the man who raised me, and I don't want you to hurt him – so don't try me. I'm perfectly capable of killing you myself."

"Mon," Raymond said softly. "I know how you must feel, and I'm sorry."

"It's so easy for you to say you're sorry," Mon said. "It's simply amazing. Hasn't anyone ever told you that? What about my father? Are you sorry about him too?"

"I am," Raymond replied. "I truly am, whether you believe me or not. I promise you–"

"Don't promise me anything, please!" Mon interrupted him. "I'm tired of your promises. Did you promise *Mamá* you'd come back too?"

"That isn't fair!" Raymond cried. "I didn't know. How was I supposed to know?"

Raymond grabbed Mon's arm, but Mon shook himself loose from his grasp.

"It's time to go," Mon said, checking his watch. "We'll leave this conversation for later. But let me give you a piece of advice. You'd better do a good job on the surgery, I warn you; otherwise the man who'll kill you won't be me – it will be Fidel Castro."

He started the ambulance, driving away angrily in a cloud of dust. The sudden acceleration thrust Raymond against his seat. He held on as Mon bounced the vehicle onto the pavement and turned left with a screeching of tires. Mashing the accelerator pedal to the floor, Mon sped around the wide turn.

"Oh, my God!" he screamed suddenly, slamming on the brakes hard. "I can't believe this."

The vehicle slid to a stop. In a daze, Raymond saw a policeman dressed in a dark-blue uniform step into the path of the ambulance, waving his arms.

"What is it, Mon?" Raymond asked with alarm. "What's going on?"

"I don't know," Mon replied. "Maybe the road is closed."

CHAPTER XII

With growing concern, Raymond stared at the mismatching pieces of the scene in front of him. A black-and-white police car with flashing lights blocked their path. By the side of the road, in the tall grass, was a stopped bus. Beyond them, by a clump of oak trees, two men argued heatedly, surrounded by a crowd of interested onlookers, which Raymond identified as the bus passengers

One of the men was the bus driver, Raymond recognized him by his slate-gray uniform and matching cap. He was tall and lanky, with a bulbous nose and a droopy moustache. The other man was a short and stocky *guajiro*, a peasant; he wore a large straw hat and faded khaki shirt and pants. Two policemen in dark-blue uniforms tried to separate them.

"What's going on here?" Raymond asked. "An accident?"

"Who knows?" Mon shrugged.

Raymond pointed at the two men. "Who are those people?"

"Don't you know?" Mon gave him a mocking smile. "I thought you knew it all. Guess."

"One has to be the bus driver, and the other I don't know. He looks like a *guajiro*."

"You're so smart!" Mon made fun of him. "But then you can make one out by the uniform, and, *carajo*, everyone is a *guajiro* outside of Havana, didn't you know that?"

"Don't be nasty, Mon. Relax."

Mon looked at him with smoldering eyes, saying nothing.

A tall red-haired cop with dark glasses perched atop a large hooked nose approached the ambulance. He had a ruddy complexion and sported a bushy moustache. The cop smiled, displaying large square yellow teeth.

"What seems to be the trouble, officer?" Mon asked him. "Why did

93

you stop me?"

"There's been an accident. We might need you to take someone to the hospital. Is either of you a doctor?"

"We both are," Mon answered. "Where's the patient?"

"There." The cop pointed to the two men arguing.

Raymond and Mon looked briefly at the men and then back at the cop, uncomprehending.

"The stocky one," the policeman explained. "He claims the driver of the bus ran him down."

"I see," Mon commented. "He seems fine to me."

"To me too." The policeman nodded. "But he's a comrade, so we have to listen to him. He says he's hurt and won't be able to work. He wants the driver to give him money. Otherwise, he'll accuse him of running him down with the bus on purpose."

"What does the bus driver say?" Raymond asked.

"He says he's not at fault," the cop answered. "He claims the *guajiro* crossed the road without looking. He says he tried to stop but couldn't."

"What actually happened?" Raymond asked.

"The *guajiro* was hit in the leg by the bus."

"What are we supposed to do, officer?" Mon asked sharply. "We're on the way to the hospital to pick up some medicines. We're in a hurry."

"You could check the man and tell me how badly-hurt he really is." The cop made a funny face, wrinkling his nose as he did so, as if he had suddenly smelled something foul. "I'm *Teniente* Antebi from the Varadero police force. If he's hurt, take him with you to the hospital. That's where you're going, anyway, aren't you?"

Raymond and Mon nodded.

"If he's not, tell me," the cop went on, "so we can stop this endless arguing. It's getting on my nerves."

"*Está bien*," Mon replied. "Sounds good to me. Let's check him out."

Lieutenant Antebi walked away quickly. Mon opened the ambulance door and started to follow him. Raymond clutched Mon by the shoulder, checking his watch.

"We have a little over two minutes to go. What do we do now?"

"Check the man," Mon replied. "What else can we do?"

"We could leave."

"They would come after us, and then we'll really be in trouble."

"I guess you're right." Raymond sighed. "I'll come with you."

"Stay in the car. I'll be back as soon as I can."

"I'd rather go with you. I might be of help."

"Suit yourself."

Mon slammed the ambulance door behind him and tramped away. Raymond followed after him.

They made their way through the crowd and reached the two arguing men. Mon addressed the *guajiro*.

"Are you the man who's hurt?" he asked sharply. The *guajiro* looked at him suspiciously.

"Who are you?" he asked uncertainly.

"We're doctors," Mon replied. "We came to check you out. Where are you hurt?"

"In the leg."

"Which leg?"

"This one." The *guajiro* tapped his right leg.

"How much does it hurt?"

"A lot."

"Can you walk?"

"Not very well," the *guajiro* stammered. "I..."

"Let's check it out then," Mon said. He turned to the bus driver. "Can we use your bus for a minute, so we can check this man's leg?"

"Of course, sir." The bus driver nodded. *"Por favor."* Mon's authoritarian manner had overwhelmed the two men.

Raymond was impressed. His son definitely had character.

"Come!" Mon commanded the poor *guajiro*, who had visibly paled. "We haven't got all day."

They climbed on the bus.

"Let me see your leg, "Mon said. "Roll up your pants."

The *guajiro* did as he was told. Raymond saw a slight swelling and a bruise. They had only one minute left. Mon touched the swollen flesh.

"Does it hurt?" he asked the patient. "Or doesn't it?"

"I told you. It hurts a lot."

"It doesn't look bad to me."

"It's worse than it looks."

"Let me talk to the man a moment, Mon," Raymond said. "Maybe we can save all of us some time."

Mon looked up. "Suit yourself," he said.

"We've got somewhere to go, and we're in a hurry." Raymond smiled at the man. "Would this make you feel better?" Raymond pulled out a fifty-dollar bill from his wallet and handed it to the *guajiro*.

The man looked at the bill with surprise... and sudden interest. He eyed Raymond's wallet with greedy eyes.

"It makes me feel better," he said cunningly. "But not totally well."

Raymond pulled another fifty-dollar bill from his wallet.

"This is my last offer," he said flatly. "A hundred dollars – or the hospital."

The *guajiro* hesitated. The wallet mesmerized his greedy eyes. Raymond put it back in his pocket and checked his wristwatch again.

"We've got to go," he told Mon. He turned to the *guajiro*. "What it'll be?"

"The hundred dollars." The man grinned, showing some missing teeth. "I'm totally well already."

"Good man." Raymond patted him on the back. "Let's go."

They hurried out of the bus with the *guajiro* traipsing behind him. Lieutenant Antebi waited by the door.

"So?" he asked. "What do we do?"

"Go home," Mon said. "He's feeling much better."

Antebi shook his head from side to side, a big grin on his face.

"You two guys are miracle workers." He chuckled. "If something ever happens to me, I want you to take care of me."

"Don't mention it," Mon said. "It will be our pleasure."

They rushed to the ambulance. Mon started the engine. He started driving away and stopped suddenly, brakes squealing loudly. He turned to Raymond.

"You handled yourself very well out there," he said. "I'm impressed."

"You didn't do so bad yourself." Raymond smiled. "I'm impressed too."

Mon jostled the ambulance onto the road, speeding away with a screeching of tires. They had thirty seconds to go.

They careened down the asphalted corridor, bouncing over bumps and chuckholes. Cuban roads had deteriorated considerably in thirty years. The venerable engine wheezed with difficulty.

Raymond looked back, expecting Lieutenant Antebi or one of the other policemen to come rushing after them. Instead he saw the bus passengers filing quietly back onto the bus. The *guajiro* was nowhere to be seen. He had probably pocketed the hundred dollars and marched away as quickly as he could on his miraculously healed leg.

"Everything okay?" Mon asked.

"Everything seems fine," Raymond replied. "We're right on time. How far away are we?"

"One more turn of the road, and we'll be there."

"You always say that. How many turns does this road have?"

Mon laughed good-humoredly. It was the first time Raymond had heard him so relaxed in his presence. *Maybe we're getting somewhere,* he thought.

"One more turn – I just told you," Mon said. "We should see them any minute now."

The vehicle leaned around a right-handed curve and faced a long stretch of road. It was empty.

"They must be running late." Mon sounded concerned. "Wonder if something happened?"

"Let's hope not." Raymond sighed. "We've had enough problems for one day already. Where's the accident *exactly* supposed to take place, Mon? Can you tell me?"

"Sure. Two hundred meters down the road. *Exactly* where the road turns right again, by that clump of trees. You see them?"

"I see them." Raymond exhaled loudly, trying to calm down his rapidly beating heart. All the excitement was beginning to get to him. "Why don't we slow down a little, Mon? We're going pretty fast. They're probably running late. Let's give them a chance to catch up."

"You're right."

Mon let his foot off the accelerator pedal, and the mammoth vehicle reduced its speed to a near crawl.

"Maybe there's been a change of plans," Mon said. He no longer sounded relaxed. "Maybe someone found out about it, and the plan was aborted."

"Maybe not," Raymond said. "Listen!"

Far away they heard the squealing tires of a speeding car coming toward them. Several moments later an old black Cadillac turned the corner.

"There they are!" Mon yelled. "It's them!"

Raymond saw the Cadillac slide around the turn on smoking tires, straighten and veer toward the trees, bouncing and thrashing into the woods. A few moments later, he heard a loud crash, followed by a thunderous explosion.

"Jesus!" Raymond cried. "I wonder if they got clear of the vehicle all right. They exploded the car too quickly."

Another black car, this one an old Oldsmobile, turned the corner with a screeching of tires. Raymond and Mon almost collided with them.

Almost simultaneously, a louder horrifying explosion rocketed the ambulance, buffeting them with a gale of wind and debris.

"My God!" Raymond exclaimed. "That explosion was powerful enough to blow out the entire countryside."

Mon stopped the ambulance alongside the black Oldsmobile. Major Teceira, his face blanched, and two other men, spilled out of the Oldsmobile and dashed toward the woods.

Raymond and Mon raced after them.

The bodies of Pepe and Fidel lay together in a crumpled heap in a pool of blood amidst the mangled trees. The black Cadillac burned brightly behind them.

"Fidel's dead!" one of the men yelled. "Fidel's dead!"

"Stop screaming and give me a hand!" Mon barked at the two men, running back toward the ambulance. "Hurry!"

The two men stared blankly at Mon for a brief moment, and then ran after him. Mon flung open the ambulance door and brought out stretchers, which he handed to each of the men.

"Carry these!" he commanded them. "Quick!"

He raced back toward the prostrated bodies, the men running after him. Raymond had to admit Mon was great in crisis situations.

"Hold the stretcher!" Mon told the men. "One at a time. We'll carry

98

Fidel first."

Raymond and Mon picked up Fidel between them and deposited his limp body, with Teceira's help, on the stretcher. Fidel was heavier than Raymond thought. His clothes were torn, and he was covered with blood. He looked *really* hurt.

They placed Fidel inside the ambulance and returned to pick up Pepe. He felt equally as heavy and didn't look much better.

A police car siren howled loudly as they deposited Pepe's body onto the stretcher and carried him to the ambulance. The wail came to an abrupt end with a screeching tires and a slamming of brakes as the police car halted next to the ambulance.

"What happened?" the familiar voice of *Teniente* Antebi asked. "What's going on here?"

"An accident," Mon explained grim-faced, slamming-shut the ambulance door. "Fidel Castro."

"Where are you taking him?"

"To the hospital."

"I'll open the way for you," Antebi said. "What a terrible disgrace!"

"There's no need to." Teceira had arrived. "I'm Major Teceira from the Security Police. We'll take care of this ourselves. Thanks for your help."

Antebi gave the major a suspicious look.

"Are you sure?" he asked. "I can open a path for the ambulance. You'll get to the hospital quicker."

"We'll handle it."

Antebi hesitated still.

"We don't want to attract too much attention to this accident." Teceira tried an ingratiating smile. "You can understand that, can't you, Lieutenant? It's a matter of national security."

"Yes sir." Antebi nodded reluctantly and saluted smartly.

"Let's go!" Mon cried. "We're wasting time."

Mon climbed back on the ambulance, and Raymond followed, closing the passenger door shut. Mon cranked the engine, which caught on the first try. He mashed the accelerator pedal to the floor and slid the ambulance with a powerful roar onto the road.

"We're off," Mon said softly. "Only God can help us now."

Raymond stared at him.

"I thought you were a communist who didn't believe in God," he said.

Mon chuckled.

"I lied," he said.

CHAPTER XIII

Neither Fidel nor Pepe looked particularly impressive lying inertly side-by-side on different beds. With their eyes wide open, under the effects of the anesthesia, they resembled dead fish.

Sonia had, swiftly and efficiently, shaved-off both their heads and faces prior to surgery. Fidel's cheeks were pink as a baby's without his customary beard, nearly the same shade as Pepe's jowls. Disregarding a few minor differences in nose and chin configuration, Raymond had to admit to himself that the similarity between the two men was remarkable.

"They do look alike, don't they?" Sonia said, as if reading his mind. Her eyes darted from Fidel to Pepe with curiosity. "The bone structure is very similar – and the skin color."

"They sure do," Mon concurred.

"Amazing," Raymond agreed. "Well, *a trabajar*. Let's get to work. Hand me that blue marker, please, Sonia. We have a lot of surgery to do yet. You ready, Mon?"

"Ready."

Sonia handed Raymond the blue marker.

"Which one are you going to do first?" she asked.

"Pepe," Raymond answered briskly. "He'll be the new Fidel. He's the one people will be looking at the most."

Deftly, a product of his years of experience, Raymond drew lines quickly on both men's faces. A moment later, he stood back, admiring his artwork.

"They look like monkeys with all those blue lines," Sonia said. "What are you doing?"

"Pinpointing where to cut." Raymond grinned. "Plastic surgery by the marker – like painting by the numbers. You never painted by the numbers, Sonia?"

"No." Sonia sounded horrified.

"You want to try?" Raymond extended the marker toward Sonia. "Go ahead."

"You're nuts, Ramón!" She stood back, out of his reach. "Of course I don't want to try it. This is a serious operation."

"Let's wash our hands then and start," Raymond said, the tone of his voice appreciably colder. "And, Sonia, whatever you see in the operating room while I'm performing the surgery, however bizarre it may seem to you, please do keep your comments to yourself. Understand?" He added, in a warmer tone, "I do take my surgeries very seriously."

"Yes, sir!"

"Everybody ready now?" Raymond looked from Sonia to Mon. "Okay, let's go. Scalpel!"

He cut into Pepe's face.

The surgery took four hours and fifty-two minutes and, when finished, left Raymond totally exhausted. Mon and Sonia were a great help, one handling the anesthesia and the other helping with the operation. They were exhausted too.

There had been only one complication during the lengthy procedure. Fidel's heart skipped a beat about thirty minutes from the end, scaring all of them. After some anxious moments, Fidel's heart resumed its regular cadence.

The biggest problem was enlarging Pepe's nose to make it look like Fidel's. Raymond had to remove cartilage from behind both of Pepe's ears to reconstruct his nose. Adding fat under Pepe's eyes was simpler than expected; just a little liposuction from the waist area and a dab injected under the eyes resolved that problem.

After twenty-five years performing surgeries, Raymond still marveled at the wonders of modern science. He marveled about human nature even more. At one point during the operation, before he started cutting into Fidel, the two men looked so alike it was like seeing twins.

In the end, in spite of Raymond's perfectionist personality, he felt the procedure was a success.

"Great surgery," Mon said.

"*Gracias.*" Raymond raised his tired eyes to look at his son and was surprised to see Mon's warm and appreciative grin.

"You're a damn good surgeon!" Mon exclaimed. "If I hadn't seen the surgery, I wouldn't have believed it."

Raymond smiled, pleased at Mon's comment.

"Congratulations, Ramoncito," Sonia said. "It was a wonderful surgery."

"I think it came out fairly well," Raymond said shyly. "I'm pleased."

"You should be!" Mon was enthusiastic. "It's one of the finest pieces of surgery I've ever witnessed – maybe the finest."

Raymond was delighted yet astonished by Mon's remark. His son's behavior toward him seemed to have changed after the surgery. Mon was no longer the wisecracking and antagonistic individual he had been before.

Who knows? Raymond thought. *Maybe I've gained his respect somehow with this surgery.*

"We need to keep both men bandaged-up for a day or two," Raymond said. "And let's make sure they receive no visitors."

"That's going to be difficult," Mon said. "Fidel's a public figure. Many people will want to see him."

"Tell everyone it's doctor's orders," Raymond said curtly. "You're his personal physician, so you do it. Tell everyone it's for his own good, and that it's important he is not disturbed for two or three days. Afterwards, they'll be able to see him. Okay?"

"I'll try it."

"You'll have to do better than that," Raymond said. "It's extremely important no one sees him for a while."

"All right." Mon sighed. "I'll do it."

"Can I count on you?" Raymond stared at him.

"Tell Teceira to post security guards in front of the door and around the clinic," Raymond said. "Just to make sure."

"Will do."

"And just in case, Sonia." Raymond whirled around to face her, giving orders, as he was accustomed to. "Make sure their heads are covered at all times. Remember, Pepe is now Fidel, and though their heads have been shaved, we don't want to run any unnecessary risks."

"I'll take care of it," Sonia answered briskly.

"Fine." Raymond looked at the two men lying on the beds. "Let's move Pepe and Fidel out to the recovery room, so we can clean up all this mess. Here, give me a hand, Mon."

Raymond pulled on Pepe's bed. Mon quickly helped him.

"Sonia," Raymond continued giving orders. "Let's make sure we destroy all these photographs, please."

"Yes, sir!" Sonia's voice was terse. "Anything else I can do for you, Doctor Peters?"

Raymond stared at her for one brief moment, then laughed.

"Let's go have something to eat," he said. "I think we're all tired – and I, for one, am starving."

"So am I," Mon said. "Aren't you hungry, *Mamá*? Let's go have something to eat."

"You go ahead, and I'll clean up," Sonia responded. "When you finish eating, come back, and I'll go. We need to keep an eye on these two at all times. Isn't that right, Ramoncito?"

"You're absolutely right," Raymond answered. "We'll be back in an hour. You want us to bring you something to eat, Sonia?"

"No," Sonia replied. "I'd like to go back to the hotel and get cleaned-up first. I'll eat something afterwards."

"*Bueno.*"

As Mon and Raymond walked out of the recovery room, they ran into a concerned Major Teceira. He and at least a dozen people waited anxiously outside for news on Fidel's well being. Among the present were Fidel's two bodyguards.

"How's Fidel?" Teceira's face was paler than usual. "Is he all right?"

"He's as well as can be expected after an accident like this," Raymond said. "Yes, he's all right."

Teceira sighed, apparently relieved by the news. Raymond was unsure whether the major was putting on an act or whether he was genuinely preoccupied for Castro's welfare. He decided he didn't care. He had other, more pressing things, to worry about – such as eating.

"When can we see him?" one of the bodyguards asked. "Can we go in?"

"Not yet," Mon answered. "He's still under sedation. You'll have to wait till he comes to."

104

"It was a long operation, wasn't it?" Teceira asked. "Did everything go okay?"

Raymond wondered why Teceira was so concerned. He hadn't been that concerned before the operation. He looked at Mon, who stared back at him with a blank expression on his face. *Maybe I'm getting overly suspicious*, Raymond thought. He shrugged.

"Everything went as expected," he answered Teceira.

"As expected?" Teceira seemed nervous.

"Everything went well," Mon said. He grabbed Teceira by the shoulders and turned him away from the door. "Don't worry, *Papá*. Fidel's okay."

Teceira sat down in one of the waiting-room chairs.

"I'm glad," he mumbled. "I was really worried."

"You don't have to worry anymore." Raymond's words were spiced with a hint of sarcasm. "At least not about the operation."

Teceira nodded absentmindedly. He seemed to have other things on his mind more important than Raymond's ironies.

"We'll see you later, major," Raymond said, wondering what was troubling Teceira so much. "We're going to grab a bite to eat. We're starving. We'll be back in a while."

They headed toward the door. Mon hesitated and turned back.

"You want to eat with us, *Papá*?"

Teceira looked up at them. Outside, Raymond heard the distant wail of sirens.

"No," Teceira finally answered. "I'd better stay here, just in case."

"Are you sure, *Papá*?"

Teceira nodded, a grim smile on his face.

The sound of sirens was getting louder fast. It seemed to be approaching the clinic.

"We'll see you later, then, *Papá*," Mon said. "Relax. Everything's okay."

With a loud screeching of tires, the sirens came to an abrupt halt just outside the clinic. Raymond heard the slamming of automobile doors. Loud, hurried steps approached.

The clinic's front door was flung open, letting in the bright afternoon sunlight. Several bearded men in olive-green military uniforms barged in, carrying weapons. Everyone in the waiting room stared at them.

One of the men stepped toward Raymond. He was short and chubby, with pink skin under an unruly beard sprinkled generously with gray hair.

Raymond had never met him before, but he recognized the man instantly from years of seeing him on television, newspapers and magazines. He looked older, shorter and fatter in person.

"Where's my brother?" Raul Castro asked. "I demand to see him at once!"

CHAPTER XIV

Raymond froze, unable to speak – and so did the others. Mon's mouth dropped open; Teceira turned pale, his moustache contrasting sharply against his skin. The three men stood paralyzed, exchanging nervous glances.

"Raul, what a surprise," Teceira managed to say. "I didn't expect you to come back for a couple more days."

The short man's attention had been focused on Raymond; now he noticed Teceira and Mon for the first time. His eyes widened in mild surprise.

"Teceira! Mon!" he shouted. "Didn't see you. Sun's so bright outside. Couldn't see anything when I came in. Where's my brother, Teceira? Is he inside?"

Without waiting for an answer, he charged toward the closed door. Raymond reacted, finally, and stepped quickly in his path.

"Sorry, you can't go in," he said, his words the bland consistency of jelly. He cleared his throat. "Fidel Castro is under sedation. He can't be disturbed."

The two men stared at each other. Raymond felt Raul Castro's anger as the man's face turned redder. Two large brown freckles alongside Castro's nose attracted Raymond's attention. They reminded him of ants.

Castro's flaming eyes shifted back to Teceira. "Where's my brother, Teceira?"

"Inside, Raul," Teceira said with a weak voice. "Inside. Don't worry. He's okay."

The short fat man again charged toward the closed door, and again Raymond blocked his path.

"You can't go in, I told you," Raymond said sharply. He had recovered his poise and was in control of himself again. "Fidel Castro is under the effects of anesthesia. He can't be bothered."

The split second it took for Raul Castro to speak seemed an eternity to Raymond. Flashes of the first time he rode a Ferris wheel rushed, helter-skelter, into his mind. He felt again the same paralyzing chill in the pit of his stomach as when he dangled terrified high above the ground, gripping the open cold metal seat.

He knew well what people looked like from a Ferris wheel – ants.

"What!" Raymond heard Raul Castro's roar as if through a muffler. "Who are you? Who's this man, Teceira?"

"I'm Fidel Castro's doctor," Raymond said.

Raul Castro's face was distorted with a rage so strong, a deep crimson color drowned all the little brown ants.

"And do you know who I am, *Doctor*? You know who you're talking to? Do you?"

From behind Raul Castro, the two bearded extra-large armed bodyguards stepped forward and surrounded Raymond. They smelled of sun and sweat and were as large and as hairy as gorillas.

The two gorillas stared menacingly at Raymond. It wasn't a pleasant feeling.

"Of course," Raymond answered in a pleasant tone. "You are Raul Castro. And I'm sure you don't want anything bad to happen to your brother Fidel – or do you?"

The question seemed to take Raul Castro by surprise; he looked momentarily disconcerted.

"Of course not," he finally said. "I want the best for my brother."

"Then you shouldn't go in," Raymond explained as if to a child. "First of all, your clothes are dirty and could give him an infection. Second, he's still out under the effects of anesthesia. He just underwent a lengthy and traumatic surgical procedure and he's lost a lot of blood. If you want to add a post-traumatic incident to the surgery, and a possible infection, go ahead! He's your brother. However, I wouldn't recommend it and, furthermore, I won't be responsible."

Raul Castro looked at him dumbfounded. Obviously, he wasn't used to people talking to him like that – and even less in Cuba. The two bodyguards exchanged confused glances. Raul Castro scratched his face precisely at the spot were the two freckles were, again, beginning to reappear – which brought a relieved smile to Raymond's lips.

"Who are you?" Castro asked, apparently seeking a new line of attack since the old one wasn't working. "You're not Cuban – or are you? You have a funny accent – Mexican maybe? Who are you? And what are you doing here?"

Before Raymond could answer, Mon stepped forward and put his arm around Raul Castro's shoulders.

"Relax, Raul," Mon smiled. "Let me introduce you to *Doctor* Ramón Robles. He's a well-known surgeon visiting us from Mexico. He was with me when the accident happened. Doctor Robles did most of the surgery himself. Thanks to him Fidel is as well as he is right now."

Raul stared from Mon to Teceira to Raymond with suspicion. Teceira moved closer so that the four men were literally huddled together. Raymond hoped Raul Castro wouldn't notice the physical resemblance between him and Mon.

"I thought you had a Mexican accent." Castro's eyes appraised Raymond. Then his eyes darted quickly, focusing on Teceira. "So, is that what happened, Teceira?"

"Yes, Raul." Teceira's color was returning to pinkish. "That's what happened."

"Can you please explain all this to me, Teceira?"

"Sure, Raul." Teceira took a deep breath. "Doctor Robles and Mon operated on Fidel–"

"How come?" Raul interrupted. "Doctor Robles is not Cuban. He's Mexican. For security reasons, he's not supposed to operate on Fidel."

"True," Teceira said. "But he's a doctor and a good one. And he was available when the accident occurred. We didn't have time to ask his nationality. Understand?"

Raul exhaled loudly, weighing Teceira's comments. Everyone in the room watched him.

"Understand," he said, and unexpectedly he smiled, his face shattering into a myriad wrinkles. "I'm just tense and worried about my brother. I'm sorry."

"We're all tense and worried about your brother," Raymond said. "But he's going to be all right."

Raul Castro turned to face him. "How's my brother really, *Doctor*?"

"He's going to be fine," Raymond said. "Just fine." The fat man's eyes narrowed as suspicion entered his mind again. He cocked his head to one side.

"Sure?"

"Sure."

"That's good." Raul Castro nodded. "When can I see him?"

Raymond hesitated a moment before responding.

"Tomorrow, perhaps," he said, "or the day after."

Raul Castro stared at the closed operating room door and his eyes filled again with doubt and suspicion. Raymond could easily imagine what he was thinking.

"Actually," he said before Raul had a chance to speak. "You can see him in a couple of hours when he comes out of the anesthesia. I don't want you to talk to him, though – not yet. You can see him from the door, so you know he's all right. Would that be okay with you?"

Raul Castro was visibly relieved. "That would be fine."

"Any other questions I may answer for you, *Señor* Castro?"

"Plenty, but I'll wait till later. Right now I'm more interested in other things." He turned to Teceira. "Was this an attempt on my brother's life?"

"I don't think so. It seems to me it was plain and simple car accident. Your brother was driving. You know how Fidel is. He was playing around, driving too quickly. He took a curve too fast, lost control and crashed."

"You sure the car wasn't tampered with?"

"It doesn't look tampered with," Teceira said. "We're still checking. I believe it was just an unfortunate accident."

Raul Castro exhaled loudly. Raymond and Mon exchanged furtive glances.

"I want a full report on my desk first thing tomorrow morning, Teceira."

"Yes, sir."

Raul smiled at Raymond, and the freckles moved again on his face. This time they reminded Raymond of Brazilian fire ants, the ones that devour people.

"I'll return in a couple of hours to see my brother. Are you having a good time in Cuba, *Doctor*?"

Raymond nodded.

"Anything you need, call me." He handed Raymond a card. "Here's my private telephone number."

He turned quickly around and marched out the door, his two gorillas following close behind. When the three men were alone again, Mon collapsed against the wall. Teceira sat down on one of the big chairs by the couch, his knees wobbly. Raymond breathed deeply and raised his eyes to the ceiling.

"That was close," Mon said.

"No kidding," Raymond chuckled.

He sat on the couch and a moment later Mon sat alongside him. The three men huddled together.

"Good thing my mother didn't come out," Mon said. "She really would've been scared."

"Your mother doesn't scare easily," Teceira said. "But she would've been surprised to find Raul Castro outside, to say the least."

"Well, I'm glad we took pains to insulate the surgery room and the recovery room so well."

"*Si*," Teceira agreed. "Money well spent."

"You think he might suspect anything, Teceira?" Raymond asked. "You know Raul better than anybody here. You work for him. What do you think?"

Teceira's brow wrinkled in thought.

"It's hard to tell. He's a hard man to read. Just like his brother. But I don't think so. I think he was just concerned about Fidel. At least I hope so."

"So do I," Mon said. He looked at Raymond. "And you, what do you think?"

"I don't really know. All I could think about while he was here was his freckles."

"His freckles?" Both men stared at Raymond.

"I think about odd things when I'm under pressure," Raymond explained. "Must be a defense mechanism. Seems to work for me."

"Why his freckles?" Mon asked.

"They reminded me of ants."

"Ants?" Teceira said. "*Hormigas*?"

Raymond nodded.

Teceira and Mon looked at each other for a moment, then roared with laughter. After a moment, Raymond laughed too. Their laughter seemed to relieve the tension.

"Ants!" Mon cried.

"*Hormigas!*" Teceira slapped Raymond on the back good-naturedly, apparently forgetting his hatred for the moment. "You're crazy!" We are one breath away from getting caught, and you're thinking of *hormigas*? Ants?"

Raymond shrugged sheepishly. The men laughed some more until, finally, little by little, they calmed down. Then they were silent.

Raymond broke the silence.

"We have a big problem to solve," he said. "And we need to solve it quickly."

Both men paid attention. Teceira sat up alertly.

"What is it?" Mon asked.

"We can't allow Raul to see Pepe and Fidel alongside each other. He might tie things together. He could suspect something then."

"So what do we do?" Teceira asked.

Raymond sighed. "We're going to have to take a big risk and switch their identities now. We won't be able to wait till they recover from the surgery."

"Isn't that too risky?" Mon asked. "They are still under the effects of the anesthesia. Pepe might say something foolish and incriminate himself with out knowing. And us too."

"I know," Raymond said. "We're going to have to take that chance. You have a better idea?"

"No," Mon said.

"Me neither," said Teceira. "How are we going to do it, though?"

"First of all," Raymond said, "we can't allow Raul Castro to enter the recovery room and get close to Pepe. He might notice some small difference between Pepe and his brother, like a small mole or a scar, get suspicious and make a connection. He'll have to see Pepe, who he'll think is his brother, from the door."

"Right," Mon said.

"Second, we'll have to move Fidel Castro to another hospital before his brother returns. Hide him in some secure place till he recovers enough to assume Pepe's identity without problems." Raymond looked at Mon. "You know a safe place nearby where we can put him for a few days?"

Mon looked at Teceira. "*Papá?*"

Teceira scratched his chin.

"Why don't we take him to the Varadero Hospital? Register him as Jose Luis Tapia." He caressed his moustache thoughtfully. "How do we explain that to Raul, though? He knows there was another man with Fidel during the accident."

"Easy," Raymond said. "We'll tell him we separated them, so we could give our undivided attention to his brother Fidel. He'll probably like that."

"Good idea," Mon said.

The three men smiled.

Teceira sighed loudly and said, "I feel better already."

"Yes," Mon said. "Me too."

Suddenly, the operating room door was flung open, crashing loudly against the wall and startling them all. Sonia swept into the room, her face white. She stared at them helplessly, eyes wide open; her lips moved but didn't make sounds.

Mon rushed to her side. He held her in his arms.

"What is it, *Mamá?* Tell me. *Mamá*, what is it? Are you all right?"

Sounds finally came through her lips, forming words laden with alarm and a sense of urgency.

"It's Fidel," she said. "He's having a heart attack."

CHAPTER XV

Fidel Castro's face was dark purple; his eyes were rolled back, showing only the whites; thick spittle foamed on his lips. He convulsed violently in the narrow bed. To Raymond, he was the image of a dying man.

They rushed to his side. Raymond's foot squished on something soft. He looked down and saw, lying on the cement floor, Castro's crumpled bloodstained bandages, remnants of his surgery apparently removed by Sonia. He kicked them out of the way.

Mon took charge of the situation, and Raymond couldn't help but being proud of him. After all, wasn't Mon his son?

"Hold him, Ramón, so he doesn't fall!" he commanded. "*Papá*, grab his other arm. Good, that's it."

While Mon barked orders, he was in constant motion. He prepared a sub-clavia catheter set and applied it swiftly and precisely into the right sub-clavia vein on Castro's neck; he fixed it in place with a nylon stitch and deftly put an oxygen mask on Castro's face. Immediately, he prepared a syringe. As he tested its contents, a fine mist sprayed the air.

"Hold him so he doesn't move!" he yelled. "Hold him, so I can give him this! That's it. That's it."

With rapid and assured motions, he applied the injection at the point of the catheter.

"What's that, Mon?" Raymond asked, as he struggled to hold Castro steady. "What are you giving him?"

"A thrombolytic treatment - streptokinase with heparin."

The liquid was absorbed into the vein, and Mon removed the syringe. He wasn't done. Without stopping, he prepared a drip solution and attached it in place. The transparent liquid dripped at a rapid pace into the catheter tube.

"Come on, Fidel. *Vamos.*" Mon spoke to the prostrate body, watching Fidel's features intently. "Respond, damn it."

Raymond watched too, hardly breathing with suspense. Fidel Castro's agitated motions slowly became more normal. Pepe, in the next bed, was sleeping soundly in the midst of the commotion. *That's good*, Raymond thought. *That's one less problem for us to deal with right now.*

"The kinase is going to take a punch at his heart and raise his blood pressure again," Mon explained.

The monitoring equipment which a moment earlier had been showing an infarct wave, turned more normal as its indicators registered more acceptable levels.

Raymond saw the heartbeat line turn less erratic first and then more rhythmical. He checked the numbers. Blood pressure: 100 over 50; heartbeat: 127; Oxygen: 95% of saturation.

"What do we do now?" Raymond asked.

"We need to stabilize his blood pressure further." As he spoke, Mon switched to a new solution. "We need to bring him down to 100 over 60, minimum."

A few seconds later Fidel Castro's blood pressure was at 113 over 65, according to the monitoring equipment; his heart showed a regular rhythm pattern.

"He's responding well," Mon said.

"On the screen, Raymond could see the beating image of Fidel Castro's heart and the outline of his circulatory system.

"The solution I injected has a trace in it," Mon explained to Raymond. "That way we can photograph inside his veins and arteries. You ever see this before? Watch what happens!"

The constricted arteries slowly began to expand, and after a few minutes they were nearly twice the size they had appeared at first on the monitor.

"Amazing, isn't it?" Mon commented.

Raymond nodded his agreement. He had seen similar procedures performed twice before but neither in such dramatic fashion nor with so much at stake. He noticed for the first time that neither Teceira nor Sonia had left the room and both were watching in awe.

Mon smiled at Teceira. "What do you think, *Papá*? I bet you've never seen anything like this before."

"No, I haven't." Teceira shook his head in wonder. "As you said – truly amazing."

"You, *Mamá*?"

"Incredible."

"Works like a roto-rooter – that machine plumbers use to clean clogged pipes." Mon laughed. "Except it's chemical instead of mechanical. But the ultimate result is the same. It destroys all obstructions and leaves the pipes squeaky clean. See the monitor? Before, Fidel's arteries were narrow because the walls were built up with atheroma and fatty deposits; blood couldn't flow – which caused the thrombosis or heart attack. Now look at them! They are much wider, because they are clean, and blood can flow easily."

"How long will this procedure last?" Raymond asked. "A week? A year? Ten years?"

"It will last 3 to 5 years. Sometimes, if you follow a good diet low in fats, forever. I have a patient like that. Did a similar procedure on him ten years ago, and he's doing great. But he follows a very strict diet and exercises regularly."

"Who says medicine isn't advanced in Cuba?" Teceira shrugged his shoulders. "We just witnessed a miracle."

"There are other procedures too, *Papá*," Mon said. "The one I did was the most expedient. Had it failed, I would have had to do open heart surgery on him. And that would've been a real problem." Mon sighed. "I'm not even sure we have all the equipment I need here."

"Good thing the procedure worked then," Raymond said. "We have plenty of problems already."

"You're right." Mon nodded. "Open heart surgery has a longer recovery period too. It would have presented a serious threat to our plans. Fidel wouldn't have been able to switch identities with Pepe for quite some time."

Teceira remained silent a moment, pondering. "So that's it with Fidel? He's okay now? You don't have to do anything else to him?"

"I may have to repeat the treatment. Apply more kinase later. We'll see. This procedure usually works with only one application – about 95% of the time. But sometimes we have to do it again."

"What about recovery?" Raymond asked.

"He'll be better than ever within twenty-four hours."

Mon checked with obvious approval the numbers on the screen, which shot up during the procedure, and were now coming down. He disconnected the catheter. A moment later, Raymond noted with relief that the numbers were within normal range again. Blood pressure: 135 over 85; heartbeat: 70; oxygen: 95%. The kinase was working fast.

Mon saw Raymond looking at the numbers.

"That's as normal as we can ever hope for him," he explained. "Blood pressure a little too high and heartbeat a little too fast. That's normal for him. He's lived a tough life. He's had a lot of wear and tear. His circulatory system is like an old boxer. His heart muscle has taken a lot of hard punches."

"500 mgs of kinase could have knocked him out for good," Raymond said. "Yet he's still alive. He's a strong man."

"He's pretty strong. I gambled on that. We needed a quick response, so I took a calculated risk."

"You did terrific, Mon. Nerves of steel. I'm impressed."

"*Gracias.*"

Sonia hugged her son warmly, messing his hair and kissing him.

"He's a wonderful doctor! Isn't he? I'm so proud of him!"

Teceira hugged him too.

"Yes, he is," he said.

Raymond felt a slight pang of jealousy and envy. He wanted to hug Mon too, tell him how proud he was, but he didn't. He felt like an outsider. Maybe he was Mon's biological father, but he was not part of the family at least not here and now.

"What's this, a family reunion?" Pepe's hoarse voice said. It sounded even more so, muffled by the bandages on his face. "How sweet! Do I get a hug too?"

He watched the group with woozy eyes, the only part of his face that was visible. He was coming out of the anesthesia.

Raymond checked his vital signs. They were normal.

"How am I doing?" Pepe asked him. "Will I live?"

"Odds are pretty good. How do you feel?"

"Good. Sore."

"You'll be uncomfortable for a couple of days."

"And then?"

"Then you'll be okay again. You're doing well. Great, in fact. It was a long procedure."

"Happy to hear that – even if I'm sore as hell."

"Oh, poor thing," Mon said jokingly. "Stop complaining, will you? You'll make me cry."

"What about the big man?" Pepe nodded toward the other bed. "How is he?"

"We just got a big scare with him," Mon said. "He suffered a mild heart attack. But we got the situation under control. We'll have to see how that affects his recovery."

Pepe's eyes widened with surprise, but he didn't say anything.

"Listen, Pepe," Raymond said. "We are thinking of moving Fidel out of here to another hospital. Raul Castro returned sooner than expected from Russia, heard about his brother's accident and rushed to Varadero. He was here and will be back soon. He wants to see his brother. We need you to assume your new identity now. Think you can do it?"

Pepe thought a moment.

"So soon? I don't know if I'm up to it yet."

"You're going to have to be," Mon said. "The way we planned it."

"We've been waiting for this moment a long time, Pepe," Teceira said. "We've been planning for it a long time too. I know it is sooner than expected, but there's nothing we can do about it. What do you say?"

"There's not much to say," Pepe said, "is there? I'll do it."

"Good." Mon patted his arm. Raymond and Sonia exchanged glances.

How can Sonia suspect Pepe of anything, Raymond thought. *And least of all of trying to kill us. She's got to be wrong.*

"We won't let him come into the recovery room, so he can't ask you questions," Raymond said. "We'll let you know ahead of time when Raul comes to see you, so you can pretend to be asleep. We'll let him watch from the door."

"Okay." Pepe winced. "And then what?"

"We'll worry about the 'then what' later. Let's worry about the 'now what' now."

"Okay," Pepe said. "I don't know if what you said had any logic to

118

it, but it had a little rhyme – and that's good enough for me."

"Good for you." Raymond laughed.

"Let's get ready," Mon urged. "Raul will be back any minute now. Help me wheel Fidel out of this room, *Papá*."

As he spoke, and with the same efficiency that had so impressed Raymond earlier, Mon started disconnecting Castro from the monitoring equipment. A few moments later, Mon and Teceira wheeled an inert Castro out of the recovery room.

"Check Pepe again, Ramón!" Mon yelled from the doorway. He was definitely in charge now, barking orders. "We don't want any more surprises."

Raymond shook his head from side to side in disbelief under Pepe's smiling glance, and did as his son asked. Inwardly, he was proud. Mon was assertive and confident – and an excellent doctor not afraid to make life and death decisions. Any father would be proud to have a son like him – and he was proud! Outwardly, he tried not to show it.

"Well," Pepe said. "How am I doing, Dad?"

Raymond put his stethoscope away and stared at his friend. He thought, *I definitely can't believe that absurd assassination plot. Sonia is wrong, period.*

"Well, Ramón, are you going to tell me or what? Am I going to live?"

"Pepe," Raymond said. "If I didn't know better I'd say you're as healthy as an ox."

"Now that's a thought." Pepe made a face. "I feel like a strong healthy ox… trampled all over me. Every bone in my body hurts."

"Stop complaining, Pepe. I told you already, that's the result of the operation."

"What's the result of the operation?" Mon's voice asked. He was back in the room, gathering medicines and miscellaneous objects, which he collected inside a large plastic bag.

"He's sore."

"Oh, that." Mon slammed shut a drawer and faced them. "That's normal."

"See?" Raymond said.

"I'm going," Mon announced. "My father's coming with me."

Raymond felt more than a twinge of jealousy hearing Mon refer to

Teceira as his father. "Where are you going?"

"To the Varadero Hospital. My father has made arrangements for Fidel to be admitted there under Pepe's name – well, actually under Jose Luis Tapia's name, which is the name Pepe uses in Cuba." He sighed and smiled. "I'm out of here!"

He darted quickly toward the door and opened it. Raymond and Pepe watched him. He turned. "I'll try to be back before Raul Castro returns. If I can't, you're on your own."

He closed the door and was gone.

Pepe and Raymond looked at each other, speechless.

"Just like you," Pepe chuckled. "A chip off the old block."

"How true!" Sonia smiled from the doorway. "He's just like his Dad."

Raymond looked from one to the other.

"*Si, Señor,*" Pepe added in a voice so perfectly modulated to sound like another voice he knew that Raymond felt the hair on the back of his neck stand on end. "And it's me who says it – the maximum leader in Cuba, the head of all the armed forces, the *Comandante* Fidel Castro!"

By the time Raul Castro returned, later than he said he would, night had fallen outside and Mon was back from the Varadero Hospital. He had left Teceira behind to tend to the finer details of making "Pepe" comfortable.

Raul Castro was in a better mood than before – and so were his two gorillas. All three were smiling.

"How's my brother?" he asked Raymond.

"Great." Raymond opened the door to the recovery room, where Pepe pretended to be asleep. "See for yourself."

Raul looked at the prostrate figure for a long moment.

"He looks different, somehow," he said, finally.

Raymond laughed, as if Raul had told them a joke. "Pretty different. He's in bed and all bandaged-up."

Raul Castro's forehead wrinkled in thought and his eyes squinted with speculation. He looked at the inert body again.

"No, not that way," he told Raymond. "I don't know... different."

Raymond shrugged. "People always look different when they are in bed sick," he said calmly, though his heart compressed. "In what way?"

"I don't know exactly. Just different."

"Maybe it's the perspective," Raymond suggested. "Relatives always say their loved ones look different while in a hospital bed."

The two gorillas behind Raul Castro stretched their heads to look at the bed. Raul looked again too.

"It's the fact they are in bed, unable to move." Mon spoke for the first time. "I find Fidel different in bed too. He's so active usually, always in motion. To see him in bed, not moving…"

Raul nodded. "That's probably it."

The gorillas behind him nodded too.

"Don't worry, Raul." Mon smiled. "Fidel will be out of here making his famous *mojitos* in a few days."

"Is that true, *Doctor*?"

Raymond nodded. "That's true. He'll be up and around in a week or so. Maybe sooner."

"All right, then." He seemed content. "Should we move him to a better hospital?"

"And create an international incident and have Cuba flooded with newspapermen claiming that Fidel is dying?" Mon said loudly. "I don't think so. Here we can treat him well, and we can control the news."

"And you, what do you think, *Doctor*?"

"Makes sense to me. It's easier to treat your brother here alone than with people milling around looking for a scoop."

"I agree too," Raul Castro said. "We'll keep it quiet. I'll have the access road to this facility cordoned-off, so no patients wander in, and post some guards around the perimeter for security purposes. For your own protection, as well as my brother's. Okay?"

"Okay," Mon said.

Raymond simply nodded.

A moment later, Raul Castro and his two gorillas had disappeared into the warm moonless night.

Less than an hour later, Teceira returned, looking concerned. He put a finger to his lips in the universal sign of silence, so Pepe and Sonia wouldn't notice, and motioned Mon and Raymond outside. They stepped past the two guards at the door and gathered under a palm tree out of earshot.

"What is it, *Papá?*" Mon asked. What do you want? Is anything wrong?"

Teceira nodded.

"What's wrong?"

"I don't know how to say this, son," Teceira said, and his voice cracked. "I just found out something tonight I had suspected all along."

"What?"

Teceira made a motion but didn't speak.

"You're alarming me, *Papá*. What is it?"

"Raul knows about all this."

"About all what? Raymond asked.

"About everything," Teceira replied. "The fake accident, the operations, everything. He knows everything."

"What?" Mon said. "Raul knows...." He stopped talking abruptly. "How do you know that, *Papá?*"

"I know."

"You sure, Teceira?" Raymond asked. "Raul was just here. And he sure didn't look like he suspected anything. I either don't know anything about human nature or he's a great actor."

"He's a great actor," Teceira said. "Both he and Fidel are, actually. They've spent their entire lives acting."

Raymond thought a moment. "I don't understand. What does he gain by pretending not to know? What could be the purpose of that?"

"The purpose is very simple, *Doctor*," Teceira said in a clipped and contemptuous voice. "To kill Pepe as Fidel Castro, so you Americans can be blamed, and Raul Castro can take over power in Cuba peacefully with the support of the rest of the world. That's the purpose! And by pretending not to know, he can make his move whenever he wants without anyone suspecting anything. Now you understand, doctor?"

CHAPTER XVI

A breeze rustled the trees, bringing with it the faint smell of flowers, fruits and decay. It was not a refreshing breeze, and it brought no relief to the heat and humidity stored in the night. Raymond heard an unidentifiable bird sing once and several crickets chirp in response. Then it was quiet again. But it wasn't a real quiet, like when one closes a door and is quiet; it was more like the quiet of the sea, where on the surface everything seems quiet but underneath unknown entities of varying sizes are wandering about, watching and waiting.

"I understand," Raymond said.

"So what do we do?" Mon asked. "What *can* we do?"

"We need to move Pepe to a safe place as soon as we can," Raymond said. "But we can't do it now. First, he needs a couple more days here to be able to recover fully and, second, we are surrounded by Raul Castro's guards – who could stop us if they think we suspect anything."

"True," Mon said.

Teceira scratched his chin. "I have another idea. I don't think anything's going to happen for at least a couple of weeks. Raul is not going to do anything just yet."

"How do you know that, *Papá*?" Mon wondered. "Or are you guessing?"

Teceira hesitated.

"And how do you know about all this anyway, Teceira?" Raymond asked. "Who told you Raul Castro was planning anything?"

"Yes, who, *Papá*?"

"I can't divulge that information." Teceira breathed deeply. "But it comes from a very reliable source."

"And is your source positively sure?" Raymond asked.

After a moment's hesitation, Teceira said, "Not one hundred percent sure. But my source is usually right about these things."

"So what's your idea, Teceira?" Raymond asked, a tone of impatience creeping up in his voice. "You said you had an idea. What is it? Tell us."

"I'll tell you. Let's assume Raul won't act for a couple of weeks or so –"

"Why two weeks, *Papá*?" Mon interrupted him. "Why not three or one or four?"

"Because Raul will want to make sure his brother is out of the country and all right before he makes his move." Teceira spoke patiently. "And it's going to take two weeks for Fidel to leave the country."

"I see." Raymond was beginning to understand. "Is Fidel your source?"

"I told you I can't tell you who my source is," Teceira said with irritation. "I gave my word I wouldn't tell."

"All right," Raymond said. He let out his breath with a loud noise. "Let me ask you another question then. Does Fidel know?"

"He probably does," Teceira said after a brief hesitation.

Raymond and Mon exchanged glances but neither spoke.

"Saturday, two weeks from now, on a Mexicana return flight to Mexico City, one Ramón Robles – you – and one Jose Luis Tapia – Fidel – are scheduled to leave Cuba." Teceira continued speaking, then paused and looked first to Mon and then to Raymond. "Both you and Fidel should be on that plane."

"That's your idea, Teceira?"

Teceira shook his head no. "That's only a part of it. My idea is that between now and then we use our time wisely and do some detailed planning."

"To do what?"

"To leave Cuba, all of us – escape. You never heard that word before, *Doctor*?"

"In Miami, all the time. South Florida is full of escapees from many countries, Cuba foremost among them."

"How would we leave Cuba, *Papá*?"

"By plane, son. I can arrange it so you can enter the military airport base in Matanzas. I can arrange it also so we can steal a plane. You are a pilot, son. You'll fly us out."

"Not a bad idea, *Papá*," Mon agreed.

"What plane do you have in mind?"

"The same you used to fly – a Mig 29."

"Who'll be going?"

"We will – you, your mom and I."

"And Pepe?" Raymond was alarmed about his friend. "He's not going with you?"

"No. He'll stay. That's what he wanted, isn't it?"

"Shouldn't we ask him that?" Raymond spoke with a curt voice. "It should be his decision. I'm sure Pepe wasn't counting with potentially being assassinated when he agreed to switch identities with Castro."

"I already did," Teceira said. "Pepe wants to stay."

"But he'll be killed if he stays," Raymond said with annoyance. "Isn't that what you said? Isn't that the reason behind all this planning? That he'll be killed if he stays?"

"Maybe not." Teceira smiled. "Maybe not. Besides, that's what he wants to do. We must respect his decision."

"Maybe not?" Raymond asked. He exchanged glances with Mon and glanced back at Teceira. "What do you mean?"

"Pepe won't get killed if we neutralize Raul Castro first." Teceira spoke slowly, enunciating his words clearly, and investing them with a heavy and sinister meaning. "You understand me, *Doctor*?"

Both Fidel and Pepe recovered quicker than expected, which allowed the group to concentrate on planning the escape. After discussing logistics several times, they decided to postpone their escape till after Fidel and Raymond left Cuba. They figured they could count on another two to three weeks while Fidel settled in Mexico and Raul was satisfied everything was in order before any action was taken. However, they didn't want to take unnecessary chances.

Sonia was chagrined about leaving Cuba without taking some of her most prized personal effects, at least, and wanted to return to Havana to pack. Teceira was opposed, arguing it would attract attention and might raise suspicions. Ultimately, Teceira's arguments prevailed and she, reluctantly, didn't go.

Raymond and Mon checked Fidel and Pepe twice a day. They were astounded by how much each looked and acted like the other before the operation. It was as if each man had assumed the identity of the other, in appearance as well as in mannerisms and gestures. Even their voices had changed.

Raul Castro visited his "brother" daily. He was allowed to talk to Pepe under the vigilant eye of Mon or Raymond, whoever happened to be around at the time. If he knew anything about the switch, he didn't show it. Occasionally, he would consult his "brother" on policy decisions and other state matters and actions. Pepe would make a suggestion sometimes, if he thought the topic was safe enough, or, more often, would delegate the decision – if any – to Raul.

Castro didn't complain anymore about his brother looking different and, in fact, complimented Raymond and Mon repeatedly about how well, and healthy, he looked.

"Thank you," Raymond would say, nearly always wondering about the veracity of what Teceira had told them. *Did Raul Castro know or not?* Sometimes, Raymond thought he detected a fine irony in Raul's comments, but other times he was certain Raul was being honest. And never once, as far as he knew, did Raul visit his real brother in the hospital. *If he knows*, Raymond thought, *why doesn't he visit his brother?* In the end, Raymond didn't know what to think.

Sonia was sad. One afternoon that Teceira and Mon had gone out for provisions, Raymond found her crying in the clinic's dining room.

"What is it, Sonia?" he asked her. "Are you ill?

"I'm afraid."

"What of?"

"I don't know. I'm just afraid. I feel something's wrong."

"Is this another one of your feelings?"

"I guess."

Raymond laughed it off and tried to calm her down, but deep down he felt the same way. Something was definitely wrong – but what?"

At 7 a.m. on the scheduled Saturday, Mon, Sonia and Raymond drove to the Matanzas hospital to check out "Jose Luis Tapia" and drive him to Havana to board their plane. The flight to Mexico left at noon and they had a two to three hour ride to the capital. Teceira stayed behind to make some last minute arrangements at the base and to monitor Raul Castro's visit, he said.

Everything went without a glitch at the hospital. By 8 a.m., after checking Fidel out of his room and having a typical Cuban breakfast of orange juice, bread and butter – well, actually bread only because there was so little butter it wasn't enough to go around and Fidel ate it all – and *café con leche*, at the sparse and dismal hospital cafeteria, they were on their way. Fidel was as loquacious as ever, talking incessantly during the entire trip – except he didn't sound like himself but like the old Pepe. Raymond thought it was weird. He had performed many plastic surgeries, but never one exactly like this one.

Seeing Rancho Boyeros airport again brought back a myriad of memories to Raymond, and a lingering feeling of impending doom. Sonia turned quiet and looked sad; her eyes were moist. Mon was his usual alert and observant self.

The new Pepe was in great spirits, jovial and healthy-looking. Dressed in a cotton plaid shirt and chinos, he looked like a man about to go on vacation – which he was. Raymond couldn't believe that a little more than two weeks ago he had been on the verge of dying.

"I'm looking forward to my retirement," Fidel said expansively, a big smile on his freshly-shaven face. "It was about time."

"Call me if you need anything," Mon said to him. "You've got my number."

Raymond winced when he heard that. Unless that call was forwarded to Miami, he didn't understand how Fidel would be able to talk to Mon. He suspected Mon was just being polite, but somehow Raymond didn't like his saying that. And he liked even less Mon's friendly tone and offer of help. Ever since his arrival in Cuba, Raymond had been caught in a thickening web of lies, half-lies, and innuendos. It was utterly distasteful to him to witness the graffiti of deceit in the words of his own son. He longed for the controlled security and plain life or death objectivity of the operating room.

A teary-eyed Sonia and a solicitous Mon accompanied Fidel and Raymond to the crowded ticket counter. A sprinkling of animated sun burnt tourists with colorful duffel bags waited patiently alongside rows of eager Cubans carrying an assortment of large string-tied cardboard boxes and cheap plastic bags. *What a contrast*, Raymond thought. *The possessions of a lifetime carried in dilapidated cardboard boxes alongside expensive bags stuffed with souvenirs. The permanent and the transient – only which was which?*

"Well, you're leaving me again," Sonia told Raymond with a flat and tiny voice. Raymond's throat felt suddenly tight and dry. "It seems like *déja vu*, isn't that the French word for it?"

"It is," Raymond said with sudden resolve. "But I'm not."

"You're not what?" Fidel turned around, a puzzled expression on his face.

"I'm not leaving Cuba with you. You mind going to Mexico alone? I'll take another flight later in the week."

"Why?"

Raymond felt Mon's curious eyes on him, and Sonia's intense glance. Fidel's face was impassive, a slight amused smile on his lips.

"I want to make sure Pepe's all right before I leave."

Castro pondered a moment, and then shrugged.

"Suit yourself. I'm out of here." He chuckled. "No, I don't mind going alone. They'll be waiting for me at the Mexico airport anyway, won't they?"

"They will," Mon said. "*Papá* told me."

"Who?"

"The same people you know in Mexico."

"Do they know it's me?"

"No."

"Who do they think I am?"

"Pepe."

"No problem then." Castro smiled. "It seems everything is under control. Would you please help me with my suitcase, Mon? I don't want to pull a stitch carrying weights."

"Sure thing, Fidel," Mon said. "*Con gusto.*"

Mon picked up the single black hard shell Samsonite suitcase and carried it to the counter. Fidel followed him. Raymond felt Sonia squeeze his arm gently.

"So you're not going after all." Her voice had a tone in it that wasn't there before. He looked into her suddenly happy eyes.

"No."

"Is Pepe the real reason?"

"No."

"What is the real reason then?"

"You know what it is."

"I need you to tell me."

"You. Perhaps this time we can leave Cuba together. I don't want to leave you again. I just found you. We'll leave Cuba together."

"You know what you're really saying, Ramoncito?"

"Yes."

"You mean it?"

"Yes."

She hugged him and kissed him, happily, carelessly and unabashed. Raymond felt his face turn hot as some people stared at them, grinning.

"People are watching, Sonia."

"Let them. This is Cuba. We are warm and loving here."

"You're also married."

"Technically, no." Sonia grinned. "Anyway, they don't know that and, besides, it won't be for long."

Raymond shrugged, resigning himself. He smiled. "You're something else."

Sonia pointed toward the counter. "What about Mon, Ramoncito?"

"What about him?"

"Is there room in your plans for him?"

"He's our son, isn't he? I'd like for him to live with us."

"Me too."

"But that might prove difficult, Sonia." Raymond sighed. "He seems very attached to Teceira for one thing, and a real son of the revolution for another."

"He has to pretend to be with the regimen, same as everybody else in Cuba, in order to survive, Ramoncito.

"It might prove difficult anyway."

Sonia's eyes watered. She remained silent, waiting for Raymond to speak again.

"But not impossible," Raymond said finally. "If there's one thing I learned in Cuba on this trip is that nothing is impossible."

Fidel returned from the ticket counter, boarding pass in hand and a wide grin on his face. He shook hands with Raymond. "Good luck to you. It's not my country anymore. You're on your own now. I can't help you."

"I know. Hope you find what you're looking for in Mexico."

"I hope so too."

"I'll walk you to the plane," Mon said.

Fidel hugged and kissed Sonia.

"Be seeing you," he said. "Take care of yourself."

"Have a nice trip," Sonia said in a neutral tone.

As Castro walked away toward the boarding gate, accompanied by Mon, Raymond couldn't help but wonder about the ironies of life. *Who said life is fair?* he thought. *Here is a world-class criminal walking away unpunished into the sunset of his life armed with a new identity and a new vigorous heart.* He would never forgive himself if this man he had reinvented with his own skillful hands, thanks to a lifetime of scientific study learned in the United States, would unleash his evil nature again in Mexico.

Sonia said something he couldn't hear, and he turned to face her. "What?"

"You're crazy, Ramoncito," Sonia whispered in his ear, nibbling on his lobe playfully. "And I love it. Crazy, crazy, crazy."

"That's what Pepe always says."

"What's that?" Mon asked, returning. "What is it that Pepe always says?"

"That Ramón is crazy," Sonia explained.

Mon observed Raymond with a serious face, although Raymond thought he detected a twinkle of amusement in his eyes. *Maybe I am making progress with my son,* he thought. *What do you know?*

Mon nodded, and his face broke into a grin. "Yeah, *Mamá*. I would have to agree with Pepe. He looks definitely crazy to me."

CHAPTER XVII

When he saw Raymond get out of the car that night, Teceira's face turned purplish red with undisguised and violent anger. Whatever pretense of civility he may have shown Raymond before evaporated. He was so furious he didn't even greet Sonia and Mon.

"What are you doing here, doctor?" Clipped words ejected from his mouth like pistol shots. "Why didn't you leave on that plane?"

"I postponed my trip."

"Why? That was a stupid thing to do. Stupid! Stupid!"

"Take it easy, *Papá*." Mon stepped in between the two men. "*Tranquilo.*"

"*Tranquilo*, Teceira," Raymond said coolly. "*Qué pasa?*"

"You're putting all of us in danger." Teceira was barely able to speak. "That's *lo que pasa!*"

"Seems to me we are all in danger, anyway," Raymond said blandly. "Isn't that what you said?"

"That's right. So why didn't you go back to your safe and beloved USA, *Doctor?*"

"I didn't want to leave Sonia, Mon and Pepe in this situation," Raymond said – and added, defiantly, "you have a problem with that?"

Teceira opened his mouth to speak, thought better of it and clamped it shut. He turned on his heels smartly and stomped out of the room. Sonia, Mon and Raymond stared after him in amazement.

"I'll go talk to him," Mon said. "It's not like him to act like that. I wonder what's wrong."

After Mon was gone, Sonia took Raymond's hand and caressed it.

Raymond noticed she had a funny smile on her lips. He stared inquiringly at her.

"I know what's wrong with Humberto," she said.

"You do?"

131

She nodded. Standing on her toes, she kissed him on the mouth. "He's jealous of you. He'll calm down – eventually."

"What is it, Sonia?" Raymond's eyes narrowed. "Has something happened I should know about? Is there something you haven't told me?"

She nodded. "I told him I still love you."

"When did you do that?"

"Before we left this morning."

Raymond whistled his amazement.

"I guess Humberto was hoping you would just go away and disappear – but you didn't."

"No," Raymond said. "I didn't."

"You made me very happy when you didn't board that plane today."

"But Sonia, you didn't know this morning I was going to do that, yet you–"

"–told Humberto anyway?" she finished the sentence for him. Sonia sighed and added, "I was tired of living a lie. Telling him how I felt was the honest thing to do."

"Right."

Sonia leaned her head on Raymond's shoulder. "I don't think I've ever loved anyone as much as I've loved you – not even Mon. And I've never loved you as much as I love you now."

Raymond kissed her head gently. Her hair smelled faintly of jasmine and love.

He closed his eyes and hugged her warmly. "I love you too, Sonia. I understand."

"I don't think you really do, Ramón. I haven't had anything to do with Humberto physically since you arrived in Cuba." Sonia raised her head to smile at him. "This morning I asked him to move out of the house."

"Move out?" Raymond raised his eyebrow.

"Leave."

No wonder he's so angry with me. No man likes to hear his wife is leaving him for another man. And he's a very proud man."

"I tried to be as gentle with him as I could when I told him. But I had to tell him. I had to be honest – for him, for me, for all of us."

"Maybe you were a little too honest?"

132

"I don't think so, Ramón. Besides, how can one ever be too honest? You're either honest or you're not. It's like being a little bit pregnant. Is there such a thing?"

"No. How come you're so wise, uh?"

She reached upward and kissed Raymond on the mouth, a long passionate kiss.

"Because I love you. I don't want to hide my love for you ever again. I've been hiding it for thirty years, isn't that enough? I don't want to hide it anymore. Can you understand that?"

"I do," he said. "And I feel the same way. Thirty years is a long time. But why is it that everyone in Cuba always asks me if I understand? Do I look stupid?"

"No." Sonia laughed, staring at him with an appraising look. "You look mocking."

"Mocking?"

"Yes, mocking. You look as if you know something the rest of us don't, and you're not going to tell us what it is, either."

"The only thing I know, which I learned a long time ago, is that I don't know much of anything."

"Well, there you have it," Sonia said with glee. "That's your answer. The reason everyone in Cuba asks you if you understand is... the fact you don't know much of anything. Did you ever think of that?"

"Oh, you're so bright," he said, and kissed her. "I don't know how I ever lived without you."

"I don't either, to tell you the truth."

They were laughing when Mon appeared in the doorway and motioned Raymond to join him in the other room. He excused himself and followed Mon. In the other room, he found Teceira sitting morosely in one corner.

Mon addressed Teceira and Raymond with a stern face.

"I don't know what the problem is between you two, and I don't care. I don't know who is right or wrong either – and I don't want to know. What I do know is that we can't go on like this. We need to have peace among us – at least until we leave Cuba. Once we reach the United States, you two can fight all you want. Right now, we need both of you for the success of this operation. Is that clear?"

Both Raymond and Teceira nodded. Raymond was impressed by Mon's ability to assess situations and deal with them. The more he knew his son, the more he liked him.

"Shake hands," Mon said.

After a moment's hesitation, Raymond extended his hand to Teceira. Standing slowly, Teceira took it reluctantly.

"Peace," Raymond said.

"Peace," Teceira said. "For now."

They discussed Teceira's plan several times during Friday and Saturday, including Pepe and Sonia on the discussions whenever possible. Sonia had chores around the clinic, and Pepe had Raul Castro's daily visits. As his facial tissues healed with each passing day, Pepe looked remarkably more and more like Fidel Castro. Raymond thought Teceira's plan was too simple and didn't allow for unexpected developments. The others agreed with him, especially Pepe. However, since none of them could offer a better alternative, they followed Teceira's lead.

Teceira would take them to the Matanzas Air Force base for a visit, and they would steal a Mig-29, which was to be piloted by Mon, and they would leave the island. It didn't sound like much of a plan to Raymond: go inside the base, steal a plane, fly out and live happily ever after.

"Just like that?" Raymond questioned Teceira on Saturday afternoon, when they were alone with Mon. "We enter the base, steal a Mig-29 and fly out? No one is going to stop us? No other planes will shoot us down? I can't believe that."

Teceira stared at Raymond, first with disbelief and then with anger

"Well, believe it, *Doctor*." Teceira had stopped addressing Raymond by his first name and now addressed him solely as doctor, in the same mocking manner he had used when they met at the Havana airport. "Because that's what's going to happen."

Raymond raised his eyes to the ceiling, showing he wasn't convinced. Teceira gritted his teeth angrily.

"Calm down, *Papá*," Mon told him. "Ramón has a right to know. It's his life too."

"What life? The good life? This man doesn't have any problems leaving Cuba. He has a plane ticket in his pocket and can leave anytime he wants. It's not his life that's at stake. It's ours."

"It's his life too, *Papá*. Be reasonable. If he's discovered he'll be shot too, same as us."

"What? You're taking his side now too, Mon?"

"I'm trying to be fair, *Papá*. *Mamá* taught me to be fair always."

"Yes, your *Mamá*." Teceira nodded scornfully. "She's very fair all right."

"What's that supposed to mean, *Papá*?" Mon's voice took on an almost imperceptible but harder edge. "Leave *Mamá* out of this. She hasn't done anything to you."

"Oh, she hasn't, has she?" Teceira's anger seeped toward Mon. "Your nice *Mamá*. Do you know what she's doing with this—"

"Stop it, Teceira!" Raymond shouted. "Leave Sonia out of this – and Mon too. You have anything to say, say it to me. Understand?"

Teceira turned red. Mon glowered. The three men remained silent. Mon was the first to break the silence.

"If you ever talk about my mother like that in front of me or anyone else, and I find out, I won't ever talk to you again, *Papá*. I swear." Mon's voice was so low Raymond had to strain to hear every word. "I love you like a father. Until two weeks ago, you were the only father I ever knew. I love you deeply. But I won't allow you to speak like that about my mother. Not ever. You hear?"

For a moment, it seemed to Raymond that Teceira's anger would get the better of him. His eyes glittered darkly as he leaned toward Mon; the muscles on his face knotted up as he gritted his teeth. He was breathing hard. With a Herculean effort, the Major controlled himself.

"Let's all relax," Raymond said in a conciliatory manner. "We're all under incredible stress. It's easy to say or do things we don't mean under stress. Why don't we discuss our escape again? Shall we?"

With difficulty, Teceira's attention turned to Raymond. He slumped back in his seat. Mon let out a deep breath and took a seat, looking at Raymond.

"Please, share your plan with us, Teceira." Raymond spoke deliberately. "How do we go into the base and steal a plane?"

"The base commander is my friend," Teceira said, after a pause. "He wants to leave Cuba too. There are a number of officers at the base who want to leave Cuba. They'll all help us, providing we promise to help them leave later."

"Well, that has a logic to it," Raymond agreed thoughtfully. "But how do we fly out of Cuba and into the United States undetected?"

"That's the easiest part of all," Teceira said with more animation. "He'll schedule the flight as a routine flight. It won't raise any suspicions in Cuba."

"I'll fly it low too, to avoid attracting radar attention," Mon broke in. "Before they know it, we'll be in international air space and out of reach; those Migs are pretty fast."

"When we radio the Miami control tower for permission to land," Teceira continued, "we'll ask for asylum."

They were silent. Raymond figured each of them was trying to imagine what it really would be like to do all that. It sounded easy as a topic of conversation, but Raymond knew unforeseen events always happened in real life.

Until she spoke, no one noticed Sonia had entered the room and was standing by them.

"How quiet you all are," she said. "Is this the calm before the storm?"

Raymond inspected Pepe's face carefully. He had done his work well. His reputation as having "magical hands" would not be damaged. Even though the surgery had taken place less than two weeks ago, the sign of the stitches was already disappearing. In a few more weeks there would be no mark left.

His friend's face was still slightly swollen, which was to be expected, but his resemblance to Fidel was unequivocal. Pepe didn't *look* like Fidel Castro; he *was* Fidel Castro. And with his two-week growth of gray unruly beard, Pepe in a uniform was sure to be the feared Commander-in-Chief.

"You've done a remarkable job, Ramón," Pepe said, staring at himself in the mirror. "You've surpassed even my expectations."

They were alone in Pepe's hospital room. Raymond could see the colors of Saturday afternoon through the open window. It was another typical blue, green and gold Cuban day – a beautiful scorcher.

"I'm glad you like my work, Pepe."

"I knew you were good, Ramón." Pepe grinned. "But I didn't know you were this good. You're a magician."

"You're going to embarrass me, Pepe."

"That would be a new one for you, Ramón."

"Tell me something, Pepe. What's really going to happen to me?"

"What do you mean, Ramón?"

"I mean you're not planning to kill me, are you? Or Sonia? Or Mon? Or any of us?"

Pepe's mouth dropped open in surprise. He glanced at his friend, speechless.

"I've been hearing some disturbing rumors, Pepe." Raymond collected the removed bandages and flung them noisily in the trashcan. "Tell me they are not true, Pepe. Please?"

"I don't know what you've been hearing, Ramón, or from whom. But I don't betray my friends, and I'm not a cold-blooded murderer. Whatever killing I've done, and I've done some, I've done for my country, and most of it face to face. Your life is not at risk, Ramón – and neither is anybody else's in our group, you hear?"

Raymond looked into Pepe's eyes. *Weird how I feel I'm not talking to Pepe at all but to Fidel Castro*, he thought.

"You give me your word?"

"I do," Fidel Castro said solemnly. "Absolutely"

CHAPTER XVIII

Late on Sunday morning they assembled for breakfast in the small sun-splashed combination kitchen and dining room of the clinic. Sonia did the cooking; she was dressed in tan slacks and a loose emerald-green blouse. The insidious yet satisfying smell of scrambled eggs and ham assaulted Raymond's senses and made his mouth water with anticipation.

Mon, wearing a t-shirt, sat at the head of the table reading an old local newspaper given to him by one of the guards. Sitting next to him, looking sleepy and disheveled in his hospital pajamas and one-week growth of beard, Pepe stared out the window grumpily. Raymond had managed to slip on a navy polo and faded jeans but was unshaven yet and felt less than energetic. Across from Pepe, Teceira, true to form, was the epitome of enterprise and style – talkative, perfectly shaven and dressed smartly in a crisply starched plaid shirt and khaki pants.

Raymond thought they formed a motley crew of conspirators.

"Everybody's going to have eggs?" Sonia asked without turning around.

The group's response was unanimous – a collective grunt meaning *sí*.

Sonia swiveled to face them, the sizzling skillet in her hand. The playful fingers of sunlight caressed her figure and tinted gold her hair as she started serving them, one by one. Raymond's blood tingled. *How beautiful she looks*, he thought. *And how sensual she is.*

Exciting flashes of the nights spent at the Club Profesionales and at the Varadero hotel invaded his mind. She was so romantic and vulnerable and exquisitely sensitive at the Club, and so bold and earthy and passionate at Varadero. Sonia was, definitely, a compendium of diverse qualities – Raymond had to admit it to himself. He wondered how many of those qualities Sonia had not revealed to him yet. However many they were, he told himself, he would be an eager explorer.

"Let's go check out the base today," Teceira said, looking at him – and Raymond felt himself blush, afraid that Humberto could see the images playing on his mind. "Let's do a dry run before the big day. That way we'll all be familiar with the layout."

"Am I invited?" Pepe asked. "I'd like to go too, if I can?"

"Sure," Teceira said magnanimously. "Why not?"

"Won't you attract too much attention, Pepe?" Sonia asked. "You look more like Fidel every day."

"We can go at night," Teceira suggested. "As the saying goes, '*En la noche todos los gatos son pardos.*'"

"I hadn't heard that expression in a long time," Raymond smiled. "All cats look dark by night."

"See what you've been missing?" Sonia said, a sly smile on her face, as she heaped a generous portion of ham and eggs on Raymond's plate. "All the old Cuban sayings."

"That's what I say," Raymond said. "I agree absolutely."

As Sonia moved away, her hand grazed lightly against his; Raymond's body prickled.

"I'll be careful," Pepe said. "I can put a hat on and cover my face."

"Good idea." Mon raised his eyes from the newspaper. "That way you won't be mobbed in the street."

"Okay, then," Teceira said, biting into his eggs. As he chewed, he eyed Sonia who had finished serving everyone and had taken a seat next to Raymond. He swallowed and added, "Let's do it tonight."

In the afternoon Raul Castro arrived for his daily visit accompanied by a TV correspondent from CNN and journalists from *El Universal* newspaper in Venezuela and the *Reforma* daily in Mexico. Luckily, Raul had the foresight to call ahead and warn Pepe he was bringing the media along. Speculations about the accident were running rampant within the international community, he told Pepe, and Fidel Castro had to make a public appearance to assure the world he was in good health.

The entourage was large and noisy and was armed with all sorts of video cameras and photographic equipment. Although Raul had assured Pepe on the phone it was going to be a quiet and intimate affair, the clinic's floor literally vibrated with the commotion; and the worrying and tense smells of sweat and adrenaline wafted through the open areas, commingling with the coppery scent exuding from the hot TV lights and the acrid odor emanating from the popping flashbulbs. Raymond surmised that nothing was ever quiet and intimate regarding Fidel Castro.

Pepe was in excellent form and gave a terrific imitation of Fidel Castro, speaking non-stop for nearly two hours on everything from making *mojitos* (the I-taught-Hemingway routine) to avoiding constipation ("Drink Cuban coffee and smoke a Cohiba cigar, and I guarantee you'll never suffer from constipation").

His most inspired comments, however, he reserved for Fidel's traditionally preferred topics – imperialism and the United States.

"The United States thinks that by making political deals with other countries in the region, such as Argentina, Costa Rica and Brazil – to name a few – they will be able to devour Cuba and make her disappear. But they are wrong! Cuba won't be devoured so easily by anyone.

"They might be able to take a nibble here or there; they might be able even to bite into a large chunk of Cuba or all of Cuba. But they won't be able to devour Cuba – because they won't be able to swallow Cuba...

"I promise you Cuba will sit undigested in the middle of the United States' stomach and give them a terrible and painful case of indigestion and heartburn.

"I promise you this, comrades: the United States might eat Cuba, but they won't be able to swallow Cuba."

Raymond watched in awe as Pepe, sounding and acting and looking like Fidel Castro, made what he considered to be inflammatory political remarks under the approving eyes of Raul Castro. *Good thing I'm a doctor and not a politician*, Raymond thought. *I don't understand anything anymore, and I don't know what Pepe is trying to accomplish by saying all these things.*

He stared at Pepe dumbfounded. Pepe winked an eye at him. Raymond shook his head from side to side. He supposed Pepe was only trying to make himself credible to Raul Castro and believable to all present. Still, there were limits…

The journalist from Venezuela was quite taken by Pepe's comments and started clapping vigorously. Two or three others in the group clapped too.

"Our country is with you, *Comandante*," he exclaimed. "Your fight against the evil forces of imperialism is an inspiration to us all in Venezuela."

The mention of "evil forces of imperialism" made Raymond think, for some reason, of the Star Wars movies and of the sinister Darth Vader.

"Thank you," Pepe said, and added in his best Fidel Castro impersonation, "To quote Dr. Martin Luther King, that great black leader of the United States, assassinated by the forces of bigotry and racism: 'We shall overcome!'"

Enthusiastic applause gushed forth from the Venezuelan delegation and was seconded by Raul Castro and one or two others in the assembly.

"Thank you," Pepe said again, beaming with satisfaction. "I'll take one last question from our Venezuelan journalist, and then we'll call it a day. It's time for my afternoon *cafesito* and my Cohiba cigar."

"And a shit, no doubt," Raymond overheard the CNN correspondent mutter through clenched teeth. "Obviously constipation is not one of his problems. This guy needs a whole box of lomotil to stop his diarrhea."

"Your accident, *Comandante*," spoke the tall and bony Venezuelan correspondent, who looked to Raymond a little like Don Quixote, although he wore a gold Rolex with diamonds. "Your accident has raised the question of your succession once more. He paused for effect and went on. "Of course, we all hope to have Fidel Castro for the next 100 years."

"Heaven forbid!" the CNN correspondent mumbled under his breath as he started putting away his notes.

"But what will happen to Cuba?" the Venezuelan Don Quixote asked. "What would happen to Cuba when there is no more Castro? What?"

"What? I'll tell you what? Nothing." Pepe looked beyond them all to the sky somewhere beyond the walls and raised his arms. "The revolution will live forever. New leaders are being formed right now in every house of every town and every province of Cuba. Once there's no more Castro, Fidel will linger on. He will live forever as the spirit of the Cuban revolution alongside Che Guevara, Camilo Cienfuegos and other great patriots. The revolution will live forever. Cuba will live forever."

Flashbulbs exploded and a deafening applause, catcalls and stomping of feet erupted from the Venezuelan delegation and shook the clinic's flimsy walls.

"What a crock of shit!" the CNN man exclaimed. "First it was Cuba – now Venezuela too? I need a drink, and fast."

They left to visit the base, which was located nearby, at nearly 10 p.m. Pepe had donned a New York Yankees baseball cap and jacket brought to him by Teceira and dark sunglasses lent to him by Mon. The ensemble, worn in the warm and humid night made him look more like a drug dealer than a head of state.

"What do you think?" he asked Raymond.

"I hope we don't get stopped by the traffic police."

"Why?"

"Because they'll slam you in jail. You look like a drug dealer."

"Funny, funny."

Mauricio drove them to the base. One thing could be said unequivocally about the old decrepit Buick: it was roomy. It fitted the six of them comfortably.

At the gate, Teceira leaned out the window to show his face; and the young guard immediately, and without asking for identification, opened the gate and waved them inside the compound.

It was mostly dark around the base, with only a few lampposts shedding a diffuse yellow light over the hangars and runways.

A young Captain sporting a pencil-thin moustache, much like Teceira's, saluted them smartly, as they bounded out of the car, and introduced him. Four tall hefty guards with machine guns stood behind him. "I'm Captain Ojeda," he said. "Follow me."

They followed Captain Ojeda silently inside the base. The guards followed behind them. Captain Ojeda stood in front of a door guarded by two uniformed soldiers. One of the soldiers opened the door.

"Please go in," Captain Ojeda said.

They marched into a small room with stonewalls and an open toilet in back. On the far wall there was a window with thick iron bars. The room looked like a prison cell.

The door closed behind them with a clang. Captain Ojeda's steps resonated on the hard stone floor. He stood in front of them. Standing next to him was Teceira.

It was Teceira who spoke.

"You're all under arrest," he said.

CHAPTER XIX

Raymond was the first to react.

"What's the meaning of this, Teceira?" he demanded angrily. "If this is your idea of a joke, it's a pretty sick one."

Teceira's thin lips parted, raising its corners slowly and deliberately, and, suddenly, Raymond was staring into a mocking smile.

"What did you think, *Doctor*?" His voice was smooth and its rising tone had a remarkable sliding quality, which conjured up in Raymond's mind the gliding motion of an Anaconda on the prowl. "You thought you could fuck with me? You thought Humberto Teceira was a *comemierda* – a stupid asshole? Is that what you thought, *Doctor*?" Teceira's voice was stretching, its undulations becoming smaller: the Anaconda had locked on a target and was viciously about to strike. "You think you could fuck my wife just like that and get away with it?" He caressed Sonia's pale and shocked face, smiling at her with teeth clamped together in undisguised and virulent fury. "This *puta* here!"

"*Papá!*" Mon screamed, stumbling forward. "What are you doing?"

Teceira shoved him back with a swift effortless motion that uncoiled the power contained in his compact muscular body. Mon stumbled back; his face white and his eyes wide open with surprise.

The Anaconda had struck.

"*Papá* shit!" Teceira shouted back. "You fucking bastard! I take you in and raise you after this asshole leaves you." He pointed furiously at Raymond. "And this is the way you repay me? You and your mother the *puta*?"

Mon straightened up and his face contracted with resolve. "Don't call my mother that name!"

He lunged at Teceira, but Sonia stepped between them. "No, Mon, no!" she yelled. "Don't! He's just hurt! He's hurt and angry with me.

Don't play his sick game."

Teceira pushed Sonia away. Raymond saw her stumble and crash to the floor. Mauricio rushed to her side to help her get up. The scene had unfolded so quickly, he hadn't had time to react. Now he was suddenly overcome by anger so intense he felt his entire body shaking with rage. He clenched his fists...

Mon's rage was more immediate. He charged at Teceira clumsily, like a bull charging at a waving red flag.

Teceira easily and gracefully hit him on the side of his face with an effortless left hook, and Mon went down.

"Come!" Teceira waved his arms at Mon who was struggling to get up. "You want to hit me? Come."

Raymond hadn't been in a real street fight in a long time. Last fight he remembered having was in high school, and it was quickly stopped after two punches. He had had plenty of karate fights in the controlled environment of the dojo or at occasional tournaments, where there were always plenty of referees present to intervene in case things became too enthusiastic between the combatants.

The inside of the cell, however, was not a controlled environment; and there were no referees present.

Raymond ignored all that, as well as the fact Teceira was a superb physical specimen in great shape, trained in both boxing and martial arts. With a roaring sound that rattled in his throat and then gurgled out totally without volition, he tackled Teceira with a ferocious thud. They crashed to the ground and rolled on the hard floor.

Raymond saw, smelled, felt or heard nothing and the only thing he could taste was his own blood when Teceira hit him in the mouth with a short, chopping right. He wrapped Teceira in a bear hug and they rolled on the floor, flailing at each other, too close to inflict any real damage to one another.

A moment later, Teceira's guards separated them; they yanked Raymond off Teceira unceremoniously and slammed him back to the floor.

Pepe, still feeble from the operation, tried to intervene but was easily disposed of by the guards and ended up on the floor next to Raymond, his dark glasses askew and his baseball cap firmly in place.

Teceira loomed tall and menacing over Raymond, his face distorted with anger.

"You want to fight with me, *Doctor*?" His voice was sibilant and full of venom. He addressed the guards who were keeping a weary eye on Raymond. "Let him go!"

Sonia again intervened, stepping between them. She was crying silently. "Stop it, Humberto!" she sobbed. "What are you going to do? Fight all of us? Fight the entire world? Stop it!"

Raymond had to admire her spunk.

Teceira breathed heavily and clenched his fists. For a brief moment it appeared he was going to hit her. Raymond bolted to his feet.

"Go ahead," Sonia challenged Teceira. "Hit me, if you want. But stop this nonsense. You're angry with me, and you're taking it out on all of them. And on your son!"

Teceira made a superhuman effort to control himself – and succeeded. He unclenched his hands and breathed deeply.

"He's not my son," Teceira said presently. "Not anymore." He pointed to Raymond. "It's his son now. Look at them! They look so much alike. Like father, like son, they say."

"You raised him, Humberto."

Teceira made a face as if he had tasted something bitter.

Raymond figured he had.

"Yes, I did," Teceira said in a barely audible voice. "And I watched him grow to look just like his father. Do you think I never noticed the similarity between them with all those pictures you have in your office? You know what it is to raise somebody else's son and be reminded everyday he looks like his father? The love of your life? *Puta*!"

Mon and Raymond both tried lunging at Teceira but were held back by the guards.

And then the incongruous happened. Teceira started laughing. It was a mirthless shocking laugh, toneless and devoid of life –the laughter of a mind going bad.

"He who laughs last, laughs the loudest," Teceira blurted in between waves of laughter. "Isn't that how the saying goes? You all know the saying, don't you? Well, I'm laughing now!"

No one spoke. All eyes were riveted on Teceira.

"Enjoy what you can tonight," Teceira went on, his words coming out of his mouth like hiccups as the sound of his laughter bounced coldly against the walls and was absorbed by the icy cell. "Because tomorrow is judgment day."

"What do you mean by that, Humberto?" Sonia asked with a quivering little voice. "What do you mean by judgment day?"

"I mean tomorrow at first light all of you will be tried as spies and shot by a firing squad for treason!"

Sonia's knees buckled and her body sagged. Raymond gently held her upright. Mauricio stood on her other side, looking at her with sympathetic eyes.

"Humberto, you'll shoot your own family?" Sonia's voice sounded terrified. "Just like that?"

"You're not my family anymore. As for you, *Doctor*, I gave you a chance to leave and you didn't take it, so fuck you too." His laughter stopped and his voice was suddenly dark, almost sad. "No, Sonia, you're not my family anymore."

"After more than thirty years together, we're not your family anymore?"

"That's right. You're not."

"Even your son? I know you're angry with me – I can understand that. But your own son? Mon is not your family anymore?"

"I told you already. He's not my son anymore." He glanced at Raymond with hard dark eyes. "The moment this man entered our lives again everything changed. I was a fool to have gotten involved in this crazy scheme. I should never have done it."

"Mon hasn't done anything to you, Humberto," Sonia pleaded. "He's always been loving and caring with you. He's always respected you and thought of you as his father."

"*Mierda!*" Teceira roared. "Enough of this *mierda*. Mon knew about you and this guy here, and he didn't tell me. He's just as bad as you two. He betrayed me too."

"He didn't–" Sonia started but was interrupted by Mon's soft, hurt voice.

"Stop it, *Mamá*. It's no use. Stop it. Don't beg."

No one spoke and an oppressive silence fell on the group. One of the soldiers coughed. Teceira looked at him absent-mindedly. "Let's go," he told the soldiers in a toneless voice.

Without a word, he walked to the door, his heels gently slapping the stone floor. Captain Ojeda and the four guards followed him, their heels beating the same tune. One of the guards opened the cell door, and the silent group marched through. The door clanged shut. Raymond heard the sound of keys as it was locked.

Raymond sat, silently, with his back to the wall; the others, one by one, followed his example, and so they were all sitting Indian file against the wall, staring at the door.

"At least, we'll die together," Sonia, said, sobbing quietly.

Mon hugged her, trying to calm her down. Pepe slammed his fist on the floor.

"And I didn't do anything," he said. "I couldn't. I was so drugged up."

"I didn't do anything either," Mauricio said with a tiny voice. "I was afraid."

Everyone stared at him in silence. Pepe, who sat next to him, tapped him on the back gently.

"It's all right," he told Mauricio. "It's all right. We are all afraid sometimes."

"At least we'll die together," Sonia said again, as if repeating a prayer.

"No one's going to die," Raymond said sharply, raising his head. "At least not yet."

Pepe and Mon looked at him. Sonia kept her head on Mon's shoulder. Mauricio's head was between his legs, his eyes fixed on the floor.

"What do we do now, Ramón?" Pepe asked. "What can we do?"

"I'll tell you what we'll do," Raymond said, suddenly standing. "Stop moping around and listen up! No one's going to die. We're all getting out of here."

Sonia raised her head and stared fixedly at Raymond. Her green eyes glistened in the semi-darkness. "How, Ramoncito?"

"I'll tell you how," Raymond said, and smiled at her. "I have a plan. Let me tell you what we're going to do. Is everybody listening?"

CHAPTER XX

When Major Teceira, Captain Ojeda and their four henchmen opened the cell door at daybreak, they stared with incredulity at Raymond who faced them, flanked by a tall imposing man dressed in olive fatigues they knew only too well.

"*Comandante!*" Captain Ojeda stood at attention, clicking his heels in a smart salute. The four guards did the same. "What are you doing here? How did you get in this cell?"

"Shut up, *estúpido!*" Pepe screamed in his best Fidel Castro imitation. He pointed at Teceira and screamed. "Arrest that man! He's an enemy of the *Revolución*. He was trying to have me killed."

"He's not really Fidel Castro," Teceira blurted out. "He's Pepe Orozco, a Cuban dissident."

Captain Ojeda looked from one to the other in confusion.

"A Cuban dissident?" Captain Ojeda made an unbelieving face.

"I mean, Jose Tapia, a Mexican tourist," Teceira hastened to clarify the situation, succeeding in making it more confusing to Ojeda still. "That's who he is in Cuba."

"A Cuban dissident and a Mexican tourist?" Captain Ojeda repeated the words slowly. "Our *Comandante?*"

"He's not our *Comandante!*" Teceira screamed, sweat forming on his forehead.

Ojeda and the guards looked from him to the imposing figure of Fidel Castro, standing before them. It was obvious to everyone present, including Teceira, what the Captain was thinking.

As if Captain Ojeda needed more encouragement, Pepe intervened forcefully with exquisite self-assurance and impeccable timing.

"Arrest this *loco!*" Fidel Castro's voice boomed in the small cell with a magnificent resonance. "At once!" And for good measure, he added, "And call my brother, Raul! Ask him to come here

149

immediately."

Teceira realized he was lost. Raymond had to admire both Pepe's powers of improvisation and Teceira's quick reflexes.

Before anyone could react, he yanked a machine gun from one of the guards and pointed it at the group.

"Hold it, everyone," he said. "No one is going to arrest me. Don't move or I'll shoot!"

There was a tense silence. Raymond stepped forward until he was a foot from the nozzle of the gun.

"If you shoot us, the other guards will come and shoot you," he told Teceira. "Besides, what are you going to do? Kill nine of us?"

Teceira's eyes blinked rapidly; Raymond could tell he was processing information and calculating his chances of escape.

"There's one way you can escape," Raymond suggested, reading his mind. "Only one."

"And which way is that?" Teceira stared at Raymond.

"Lock us in the cell and leave," Raymond said. "We'll give you ten minutes to get away before we call for help."

"You think I will trust you?"

"I give you my word

Teceira blew air through his lips in the universal gesture of disbelief. "I don't trust you, *Doctor.*"

"And me, Humberto?" Sonia said with a sad voice. "Do you trust me?"

Teceira opened his mouth as if to scream at Sonia, then said softly, "Even less, Sonia."

There was another tense silence. Then Teceira moved with quick resolve. It was obvious he had made up his mind.

"All right," he said. "Get in the cell, all of you. Give me the keys, Ojeda." He looked at Sonia. "You'd better keep your word this time, Sonia, because if you don't, I'm coming back to kill you all. And you know who's the one I'm going to kill first? Mon! You hear?"

Sonia shivered.

Teceira stepped through the cell door and slammed it shut. A moment later, Raymond heard the metallic sounds of the key on the lock.

"I'll leave the keys outside!" Teceira yelled. "And remember what

I told you, Sonia. You betray me, and I'll come back to kill Mon and you and everyone. And don't think you can escape me. So you'd better keep your word. I'll be around watching you."

Then Raymond heard Teceira's rapidly disappearing steps down the hall, and he was gone.

They huddled in Captain Ojeda's office. Raul Castro sat grimly behind the desk and Raymond, Mon, Sonia, and Mauricio sat attentively in the visiting chairs. Pepe stood, leaning on the desk.

"I knew all about this crazy plastic surgery idea from the beginning," Raul explained. "My brother, Fidelito, wouldn't do anything so crazy without consulting me."

"But then," Raymond said. "Why didn't you say anything? We were worried about you."

"I was worried about you," Raul Castro told Raymond. "You have balls of steel, *Doctor*. That day I came to the clinic and you stopped me at the door, I wanted to kill you."

"You knew then?"

"Of course."

"So why didn't you say so?"

"Many reasons."

"Like what?" Raymond insisted.

Raul Castro breathed heavily. "Teceira, for one. We didn't want him to know. We suspected he was involved in some plot against us. We couldn't trust him."

"Was he?"

"All the way to his neck. He tried to get Ojeda involved too. And some of the officers here at the base."

"Did he succeed?"

Raul Castro smiled. "They swear he didn't. I don't know for sure."

"So what do we do now?" Raymond asked.

"You must leave the island," Pepe said. "Teceira is out there somewhere and dangerous."

"How do we do that, Pepe?" Mon asked. "You'll give us a plane to steal?"

"I'm afraid we can't do that," Raul Castro said. "Wouldn't look good on us. This situation is delicate enough as it is – and potentially embarrassing to us. You are lucky I let you leave Cuba alive."

"Why do you let us leave Cuba alive?" Raymond asked.

Raul Castro made a motion toward Pepe with his head. They all looked at Pepe.

"It was a deal we made," Pepe explained. "I'm a man of my word, Ramón. Something happens to you, any of you, and the same thing happens to Fidel in Mexico." He grinned. "I believe it's called a Mexican stalemate or something like that, isn't it, Mon?"

"I guess." Mon made a face. "I don't really know."

"What do we do then?" Raymond asked.

"You can go by sea," Pepe said. He stuck his hand in his pocket and brought out a wad of dollar bills, which he handed to Raymond. "Remember Juan, in Regla?"

"Yes, of course," Raymond said.

"There's a place in Regla where contraband boats leave for the United States. There's one leaving tonight. I suggest you hurry."

"Just like that?" Sonia said.

"I'm afraid time is of essence," Raul Castro said.

"That's right," Pepe said. He turned to Mauricio. "What about you, Mauricio? Will you be leaving too?"

"Yes, Pepe," Mauricio said. "I've been wanting to go to the United States for a long time. I don't have a family. Not even a steady girlfriend. I'd like to go too."

"All right then." Pepe turned to Raymond again. "I gave you enough money to pay the fare for the four of you. Just give it to the man who's going to take you across when he asks, understand?"

"Understand."

"You must get going."

Raymond and the others stood. Pepe hugged each in turn until he came to Raymond. He gave him a strong hug, as if he didn't want him to go.

"I believe this is good-bye," Pepe told Raymond. "I doubt we'll see each other again. Good luck to you."

"Good luck to you too, Pepe. You'll need it."

Raymond and the others walked quickly toward the door. Pepe called his name when he reached the door, and Raymond turned.

"Yes, Pepe?"

"And don't you forget it," Pepe said, a lopsided grin on his Fidel Castro face. "You are still, and will always be, my best friend."

CHAPTER XXI

They sped toward Regla in the moonless night, the old Buick groaning and creaking at every bump and turn of the dark and solitary road. Mauricio drove in silence. Everyone in the car was silent, each apparently content to have a moment of solitude to reflect on the day's events. No one slept either.

Mon sat up front by Mauricio, in his usual place; Sonia and Raymond sat in back. Even with the front windows rolled halfway down for ventilation, it was hot inside the Buick.

Once during the trip, as they crossed into the province of Havana, Mon turned back to ask Sonia if she was all right.

"*Sí*," she answered.

It was the last word spoken in the car until they reached Regla.

The fishing village was still asleep. They drove silently through narrow unpaved streets, illuminated only by the dim yellow lights of ancient corner lampposts. Noiselessly, except for the creaking sounds of the Buick's suspension, they glided past rows of darkened unpainted wooden houses. The faint whiff of the sea slipped through the open car windows.

The night was cooler now, Raymond noted. Although it was still pitch black, screaming seagulls announced dawn was coming. They didn't have much time.

"We must hurry," Mon said, as if reading Raymond's mind.

"We're almost there," Mauricio said.

And they were. Mauricio made one last turn into a narrow street and stopped the car in front of a house much like the others, leaving the engine running.

"It's here," Mauricio said. "19 Guevara Street."

The door of the car creaked open, and Mauricio got out heavily and walked toward the house. Before he could knock on the door, it opened and Juan came out.

"Been waiting for you," Juan said. "Pepe called ahead and told me to expect you."

"Did he tell you what happened?"

"No. I don't want to know either."

"Why not'?"

Juan laughed. "In Cuba the less you know the better it is."

"What did Pepe tell you?"

"To put you on a boat to Florida tonight. I've already made arrangements. We must hurry."

He got in the car alongside Mon, who moved to give him room; Mauricio got back in the driver's seat. After introducing Juan to the group, Mauricio drove away with Juan giving directions.

"So we meet again," Juan grinned to Raymond when he saw him. "Small world, isn't it?"

"Yes," Raymond agreed. "It's a small world all right."

"Turn here," Juan told Mauricio. "We've arrived."

Mauricio drove the Buick onto a narrow and bumpy dirt street that dead-ended facing the sea. The strong smell of sea salt and the sound of swelling waves assaulted Raymond's senses and brought to his mind a myriad jumbled pleasant memories. Mauricio stopped the car. The engine ran on and then finally gasped to a stop.

Sonia squeezed Raymond's hand; he gazed at her. She had tears in her eyes.

"What is it?" he asked her. "Something wrong?"

She shook her head no. He started to open the car door, but she held him back. He looked at her.

"All my life here, Ramoncito, and I'm leaving with nothing but my memories."

"You won't need anything where we're going," Raymond said. "Except your memories."

"I couldn't bring even one picture."

No one moved inside the car. They all listened to Sonia.

"But I'm happy," she said, tears rolling slowly down her cheeks. "I'm happy because I'm leaving Cuba with what is the most important to me in my life – Mon and you."

Everyone sat still in the car, transfixed, staring at Sonia. A seagull screamed outside.

"Maybe Pepe can help and send you some of your things," Mauricio said helpfully.

"Yes," Sonia said. "Maybe."

Juan got out of the car. Raymond opened his car door to follow him.

"Stay in the car." Juan motioned to hjm. "Better if I go alone."

"Where are you going?"

"To see Baseball."

"Baseball?" Raymond said.

Juan grinned. "The guy who's going to take you. They call him 'Baseball.'"

"Why is that?" Raymond asked. "He used to play baseball or something?'

Juan didn't answer him. He stepped over a sand dune, past some vegetation, and was gone into the night.

"I guess he didn't hear you," Mauricio said. "I don't know why they call him Baseball. I just know that's what everybody calls him."

"You know this man?"

"I know of him," Mauricio said. "He carries a baseball bat around in his boat. Maybe that's why they call him Baseball?"

"Maybe."

"I believe I've heard of this man too," Mon said.

"What have you heard?"

Before Mon could reply, Juan was back.

"Let's go," he said, gasping. He had been running. "They've been waiting for us, and it's getting late. You must hurry. If you don't go now, you'll have to wait three days."

"Can't do that!" Mon was alarmed. "They might find us."

"Let's go then! Let's go!" Juan repeated. "Hurry! There's no time."

"What do I do with my car?" Mauricio asked.

"Leave it. I'll take care of it. I don't have a car. Give me the keys."

Mauricio, almost reluctantly, did as he was told.

"Take good care of it," he said to Juan. "It's been with me a long time."

156

"I will. Now hurry up. All of you."

They got out of the car quickly and followed Juan. They stumbled after him through brushes and over a dune and onto the soft sand of a deserted beach. Juan led them to the hard sand close to the sea where it was easier to walk. They skirted the shoreline for about fifty yards, the swelling waves lapping at their feet, until they reached a cove hidden by a large dune.

Raymond saw three large motorboats filled with people pitching and yawing in the sea about twenty yards from shore. As they approached, a large unshaven man with a bushy moustache materialized from the darkness like an eerie ghost. He was carrying a baseball bat. Raymond noticed he was dressed in shorts and a torn t-shirt and wore a dirty NY Yankees baseball cap.

"Are these the people?" he asked Juan gruffly, eyeing the group with small porcine eyes. "It was about time. I was about to leave without them."

"Yes, Baseball, you already told me," Juan said. "These are the people."

Everything seemed to be either too small or too large or simply too out of proportion with Baseball, Raymond noted. His ears were unusually small, matching his skinny little eyes and tiny mouth and his small totally shaved round head; yet his hands and feet were big; and his body was extremely large and bloated, as if someone had pumped him full of air. It made his somewhat delicate features seem grotesquely distorted.

Baseball smiled at them. His large teeth were pointed, Raymond noticed, much like those of a shark or a barracuda; and although there wasn't enough light to see, Raymond guessed they were probably yellow too.

"Hurry up, then!" Baseball waved his bat with an urgent motion. "Follow me."

He trudged on the sand. They followed. He stopped suddenly and turned around, scratching his unshaved chin.

"How many are you?" he asked Juan. "Four or five? The deal was for four."

"I'm not going," Juan said. "It's the four of them."

Baseball inspected the group again. His eyes lingered on Sonia.

"Okay." He nodded, apparently satisfied. "Where's the money? You know how it is: no money, no trip. *No hay dinero, no hay viaje.*"

"He's got it." Juan pointed to Raymond. "Give him the money."

Raymond took out of his pocket the wad of dollar bills Pepe had given him earlier and handed it to Baseball. The big man counted the crisp notes slowly and carefully.

Apparently, the money was all there because when he finished counting, Baseball emitted a satisfied grunt. He stuffed the bills in his pocket and pointed to the beach.

"Go ahead!" he ordered. "Get in the middle boat. That's my boat. You'll have to get wet. We can't bring the boat closer to shore."

Raymond trudged ahead into the sea, pulling Sonia by the hand. The water was warm. The others followed.

He turned after a few meters.

"*Gracias* for everything, Juan!" he yelled. "We'll be in touch."

"Go with God." Juan waved.

Raymond heard Baseball chuckle behind them.

A few minutes later, they had climbed on board the boat and taken a seat. Raymond counted twenty-six other people aboard, ranging from small frightened children to terrified old ladies. They all wore life jackets.

"Here, put these on!" Baseball threw four dark-green life jackets at them. "If we sink, they'll keep you afloat – and the US Coast Guards won't see you 'cause they're dark."

Not a very promising beginning. Raymond thought. *Thinking about sinking.*

He did as he was told, and so did the others. Raymond heard Baseball drop his bat noisily and start the motor. The powerful roar of twin engines and the gurgling sound of the exhaust filled the air. A whiff of diesel fumes attacked Raymond's nostrils.

"Now, be quiet!" Baseball commanded. "Don't make any noise. We don't want anyone to hear us."

Soon they were underway, heading out of the calm bay into the ocean in the foggy night, chasing a hint of weakly gleaming stars. Raymond, Mon and Mauricio exchanged glances. Sonia made the sign of the cross.

With the exception of a rough patch with high waves that made the children sick, the Florida Straits were relatively calm that night. Dawn was tinting the sky pink when they arrived at a group of small deserted islands.

"We're almost on the Florida Keys," Baseball announced. "We must be extra careful now. The Coast Guard patrols this area."

He cut the speed of the boat and the noisy growl of the twin engines was replaced by a smoother insistent hum. The boat approached the coastline slowly. A deep fog rose from the water, shrouding them in a mantle of gossamer gray.

About twenty yards from the coastline, Baseball made a sharp birdlike sound. A moment later a similar bird sound echoed from the shoreline.

"It's here." Baseball grinned broadly, flashing a gold tooth Raymond hadn't noticed before. "We made it. Again." He stopped the engines and threw the anchor into the shallow waters. "You all get off here. Domingo will take care of you now."

"Domingo?" Raymond asked.

Baseball nodded. "Domingo."

"Who's Domingo?" someone asked.

"He's the other bird on shore. He'll take care of you from now on. He's waiting with a bus and dry clothes. He'll drive all of you all the way into Miami. Go! Leave the lifejackets! You won't need them anymore. You can walk to shore."

They all removed their lifejackets and one by one entered the water. They could touch bottom. The water was warm. People from the boat came into the water with them and soon the small covelet was dotted with bobbing heads walking to shore, a silent invading army of refugees seeking freedom.

Suddenly they heard a commotion. Baseball was screaming.

"So you thought you could get away without paying, uh?!" He yelled. "No wonder you didn't want to pay when you came on board. I told you, 'no money, no trip.' Now pay! Or else!"

Raymond strained to look. Others, frightened by the noise, rushed to shore, splasing in the water. A young powerfully built man who had sat silently and sullenly in the boat, argued with Baseball.

Unexpectedly, the young man shoved Baseball back and dove into the water; he was still wearing his lifejacket. He started running toward shore but the bulky lifejacket slowed him down.

Baseball's reaction was incredibly swift for someone so heavy. He yanked the anchor into the boat quickly and cranked the engine. With a powerful surge, the boat blocked the path of the young man, who changed directions and tried to swim away from the boat. It was obvious to Raymond that the young man's lifejacket hindered his motions considerably. The young man knew this too, but every time he tried to remove his life jacket, Baseball's boat approached and he had to move.

Playing a lethal game of cat and mouse, Baseball skillfully kept the young man away from shore with his boat. Every time the young man made a run for shore, the boat cut him off and he had to swim away. Exhausted from the swimming, the young man finally ceased moving and waited for the boat to approach.

Sonia, Mon, Mauricio and Raymond had already reached shore. They watched curiously from beneath a large palm tree.

"No one gets away from me," Baseball said. "No one. You tired? You give up?"

The young man said something Raymond couldn't hear but that must have been a yes because he heard Baseball say to him, "Okay. Give me your hand. I'll pull you up."

Raymond saw Baseball extend his left hand; the young man took it.

Unexpectedly, Raymond saw the blur of the bat in Baseball's right hand and heard a sickening, crushing thud as the wood struck the young man's head. The scream of the young man curdled Raymond's blood.

He saw Baseball brace himself with his knees against the side of the boat and hold the bat with both hands. Again and again the bat struck the bobbing head and with each hit the young man's screaming got weaker until he was finally silent. Raymond could still hear the thudding of the bat for a while longer until it too, finally, stopped.

He and the others watched horrified from the coast.

Baseball was breathing heavily from the exertion. In the pink dawn, Raymond could see his face glistening with sweat.

Baseball faced the coast and screamed, "That goes for all of you and your families too. Don't fuck with me. No money, no trip! You don't pay me, the only trip you take is to hell!"

Raymond, Mon, Mauricio and Sonia watched from the coast in fascinated horror as a heavily breathing Baseball headed his boat slowly back out to sea. As he was about to disappear into the fog, he turned around one more time and screamed at the lifeless figure of the young man bobbing in the water in his lifejacket.

"You can keep the lifejacket, *cabrón*! With my compliments."

Then the fog enveloped the boat and Baseball, and Raymond could only hear the diminishing sound of the powerful twin engines. In the shallow water a growing pink stain – nearly identical in shade to the color of the dawn tinting the new day – spread rapidly around the dead body of the young man in the dark-green lifejacket, his broken dreams oozing rapidly out of his blood-gushing head.

Raymond felt Sonia shiver, and he put his arm around her. She was crying quietly.

"Poor man," she sobbed. "So young to die such a violent death. Murdered like that."

"We couldn't do anything about it, *Mamá*," Mon said. "It happened too far away. I'll call Pepe on his private line and let him know about it. He'll take care of this man, I'm sure."

"Yes," Raymond said, feeling guilty nevertheless. "He'll take care of this man." He turned to Sonia. "They were too far away. There wasn't much we could do."

"Best thing is what you did – nothing! That Baseball is a crazy psycho!" a short fat man with round, horn-rimmed glasses said next to them. "This is not the first he kills like that. He's done it several times before. Always people who don't want to pay."

"Ohhh," Sonia said with revulsion.

"They don't pay, Baseball kills them," the man said. "I think he likes it too. Just to get out of Cuba some people say they have the money, but they don't. They don't pay him, he kills them. He's an animal, this Baseball. He should be locked up in a zoo someplace with the animals."

The man, Raymond now noticed, wore a pink Tommy Hillfiger sports shirts, white shorts and boat shoes. He looked the image of material prosperity. He definitely hadn't come in the boat with them through the Florida Straits.

"Who are you?" Raymond asked.

"I'm Domingo, your guide," he announced pleasantly, shaking hands all around. "Please, follow me. All the others are already inside the van."

They followed Domingo in the sand around high brushes and tall palm trees swaying in the lifting breeze to a large white van with tinted windows parked by the road. Raymond read the dark blue letters painted on the side: MEDICAL TRANSPORTATION.

No wonder the van seemed familiar, Raymond thought. *So that's how they do it. Amazing.*

"Please, go in," Domingo said amiably. "It's getting light, and we need to roll. There are dry clothes in back, if you want to change."

They climbed on board. The clothes were either too small or too large and didn't fit them. Only Mauricio found a red shirt his size and put it on. They found seats up front close to the driver and sat down. Raymond guessed the others didn't want to be seen and chose seats in back.

"Keep away from the windows and don't say a word if we get stopped," Domingo said. "I'll do the talking. For your information, you're all safe now. You're in Florida, in the United States. As Cubans you're entitled to political asylum. You are safe now."

Someone yelled with unrestrained ebullience and suddenly a tall mulatto in back exploded with shouts of jubilation. Domingo quieted him down.

"*Qué importa!*" the man said. "We're free now."

Several of the others chorused their agreement and started shouting happily too. Domingo had a tough time getting them to calm down. Eventually, one by one, they stopped.

"Takes longer if we get stopped," Domingo explained patiently. "You'll get put in jail in the Keys first, then transferred to Krome in Miami. It's more complicated. Different jurisdictions are involved. Be patient for another two hours or so and in a few days you'll be drinking Cuban coffee and playing dominoes in *Calle Ocho*."

A hush fell inside the van. Domingo started the engine and wheeled the van onto the road, facing the emerging golden disk of the sun. They were on their way.

The trip was remarkable only because it was uneventful. Raymond dozed off and woke up only when he heard Domingo's voice again.

Sonia was leaning on his shoulder, fast asleep. Mauricio slept too, his head resting against the windowpane. Mon smiled at him from his seat.

"What?" Raymond asked him, still groggy with sleep.

Mon pointed with unrestrained excitement.

"What?" Raymond repeated.

"Look!"

Raymond looked. He saw the familiar rectangular buildings and the neat red tile roofed houses silhouetted against the azure sky, its glass windows flashing orange in the early morning sun. Before he heard Mon's words, Raymond knew where they were.

"We are in Miami," Mon said.

CHAPTER XXII

As he sipped his breakfast coffee, Raymond looked through the large picture windows of his 34th-floor condominium on Brickell Avenue at the placid green waters of Miami Bay. Buffeted by the wind, the ornamental flags of nearly two-dozen countries stood in a row, like soldiers, guarding the front of the Mandarin Hotel on Brickell Key.

It fascinated him how strong the breeze blew on the bay, even in a hot sunny day like today. And it was even stronger when he stood on the balcony. The condominium was so high up the more distant boats in the water below seemed like mere dainty impressionistic brush strokes.

"Windy out today," he said to Sonia, who sat by his side watching him. He put his cup back on the saucer. "Don't you think?"

"Windy out every day." Sonia fussed over the knot of his tie, making sure it dimpled correctly. "You look very handsome in your navy blue suit and striped shirt. You look more like a businessman than a doctor. Isn't this the tie I gave you for your birthday?"

As if she didn't know, thought Raymond. *Women never forget what gifts they give.*

"Is it?" He pretended he didn't know and flipped the tie to look at the name printed in the back. He feigned a look of surprise and said, "Hermes? Isn't that a Greek god?"

"Stop fooling with me." Sonia hit him playfully on the shoulder.

Unlike Raymond, Sonia was dressed in shorts and a tank top. *She looks healthy and tanned.* Raymond thought. *And more beautiful than ever. The United States definitely agrees with her.*

He checked his watch. "Where's Mon?"

"He's getting ready," she said. "It's a big day for him."

"Yes," Raymond agreed. "And for me too."

"That was such a great idea you had, setting up your own clinic so

164

you two could work together." She smiled warmly at him and kissed him lightly on the lips. "But then you always do have good ideas, don't you?"

"Not always."

"That idea you had to get us out of jail in Cuba was incredible," Sonia said. "To have Pepe impersonate Fidel Castro like that. I wouldn't have thought of it. I thought we were going to be shot for sure."

"Pepe deserves a lot of the credit. He did a great job playing out the role of Fidel."

"Yes, but it was your idea," she said. "And your plan. And it worked perfectly."

He saw her eyes moisten and said, "Let's not talk about that – it's in the past. Let's talk about now and the future."

"You're right." She smiled again, her eyes still a little sad with the memory.

"I didn't know if the idea of the clinic was going to work, to be honest with you," he said. "A cardiologist and a plastic surgeon don't seem to have much in common."

"That's why your idea is so good – a clinic specializing in diagnostics, sports medicine and reconstructive surgery. I think it's a great idea."

"You really like it, then?"

"I love it," she said. "Mon does preventive medicine and keeps everyone in great shape and when the flesh begins to sag, you turn them young again."

"Seen from that perspective, I would have to agree."

"And I love the name you gave to the Clinic," Sonia said. "It makes me want to cry."

"Peters and Peters," Raymond said. "I must admit I like the sound of it too."

She hugged him happily. He kissed her softly on the lips.

"I couldn't have done it without you," he said. "Thank you for your support. And for giving me my son back."

"You're welcome."

Sonia looked away from him toward the Mandarin Hotel, and Raymond noticed the tears in her eyes. He hugged her gently.

"Wonder how they did the selection," he said.

She turned toward him, a baffled look in her eyes. "What selection?"

"The flags in front of the Mandarin. With so many countries in the world, I wonder what criteria they used to select only those."

Sonia started laughing, which broke the tension, which was what he wanted. He chuckled too.

"Your mind never stops churning," she said. "It's amazing the things you think about."

"You think so?"

"I think so."

They chuckled together. The doorbell sounded. "Wonder who that is?" Raymond was puzzled. "I'll go check."

It was Mauricio, carrying a large manila envelope in his hands.

"Good morning, Mauricio," Raymond said. "How was your weekend?"

"Great," Mauricio said. "I had a great weekend."

"You look like you went to the beach." Raymond grinned. "You have a sun tan."

"I did." Mauricio nodded. "I went to the beach with a friend. We went jogging and did other interesting things." He grinned widely. "It was a lot of fun. I enjoyed every moment."

"Good for you," Sonia said. "You have to enjoy life."

"That's right." Mauricio nodded. "You never know when you're going to check out. It can happen any moment, any time, any place. Might as well enjoy life while you can."

"What's that envelope you have in your hands?" Raymond asked. "Is it for us?"

"It's for you – for Doctor Peters." Mauricio handed Raymond the envelope. "They just left it downstairs for you."

"Who left it?"

"A man left it." He hesitated a moment and added, "A well-dressed Cuban."

"Anybody we know?"

Maurico shook his head no.

"I see." Raymond took the package from him. "*Gracias,* Mauricio."

"*De nada.* Isn't Mon ready yet?"

"Not yet," Sonia said. "He's still getting dressed."

Mauricio smiled. "Should I bring the car around to the front?"

"Please do," Raymond said. "We'll be down shortly."

After Mauricio was gone, Raymond closed the door and examined the envelope. It had no return address. On the front, scrawled in large block letters in shocking red ink was only his name: Dr. Raymond Peters.

"What is it?" Sonia peeked over his shoulder. "Who sent it?"

"I don't know," Raymond replied.

He tore one corner of the envelope open and glanced at its contents. There were only two items inside, which he brought out to examine – a newspaper clipping from a Mexican newspaper and a single unsigned sheet of paper typewritten in Spanish.

Raymond read the typewritten sheet first. It was very brief. "It said: "We are keeping an eye on you, Doctor. We know every move you take and everything you do, even what you have for breakfast or where you buy your expensive ties." Raymond felt a shiver run through his body and had to stop reading for a moment. He took a deep breath and resumed his reading. "Don't do or say anything about what happened in Cuba. Ever! It would be hazardous to your health!"

That was all, except for the postscript, which read: "See the attached newspaper clipping."

The newspaper clipping was from a Sunday newspaper in Mérida, Mexico. It, too, was brief. It said: "The body of an old fisherman was found dead of two bullet wounds to the head on Puerto Progresso Beach early this morning. Local authorities have traced the victim's name to that of Jose Orozco, a Mexican citizen of Cuban extraction. No motive for the strange murder has been discovered yet. Local authorities are investigating."

"You all right, Ramoncito?" Sonia asked, holding his arm. "You look pale. Any problems?"

"Nothing for us to worry about now," Raymond said, regaining his composure. "Really nothing."

He put both items inside the envelope again, which he folded twice and slipped inside his coat pocket. He would destroy it later.

Sonia was about to say something more when they heard Mon's

room door open and his steps come down the hall. He appeared in the living room dressed elegantly in a medium-gray suit, white button-down shirt and silk maroon tie. He had a smile on his face.

"Good morning." He beamed at them.

He kissed Sonia on the cheek while she mumbled in his ear how handsome he looked. He hugged Raymond.

"Ready, son?" Raymond asked him.

Since it was the first time his son had addressed him like that, Mon's answer lingered in Raymond's ears with the myriad resonant complexities of a Gregorian chant; and, as his blood tingled with a joy he had never known before, Raymond knew, finally, that everything was going to be all right between them.

"Ready, Dad."

EPILOGUE

The gray-bearded old man sat in a discolored wooden chair, his bare feet buried in the sand, fishing off the rocky shores of Puerto Progresso Beach in Yucatan. Despite the unusual coolness of the incipient day, he wore only a pair of faded and tattered khaki shorts. He was actually napping at the time. His fishing pole was securely fastened to his chair by a rope. Next to it rested a black plastic tackle box and a cooler full of beer topped with crushed ice. He brought it every day to fish. He loved the taste of the ice-cold beer when the day turned hot and the fiery Yucatan sun made his skin tingle and his mouth dry with thirst.

It was not yet dawn. The sky was dark still, although on the horizon a faint pink was beginning to spread on the gunmetal gray. The beach was deserted yet; it would fill up later when the sun came up bright and warm and enticed the families living in the area and the tourists looking for action and excitement.

Below the spreading pink on the horizon, two men in jogging suits appeared and started trotting slowly along the coastline toward the old man. The old man was fast asleep, snoring.

A tug of his fishing pole woke him up, startled. He scratched his beard and smiled.

"Ah, we're beginning early today," he said aloud. "I had a hunch the fishing was going to be good today. Yesterday was so bad."

He had gotten into the habit lately of carrying on long conversations with himself. People sometimes looked at him funny, as if he were crazy or something. He didn't care. He needed to hear the sound of his own voice.

He guessed that was because he had spent most of his life surrounded by people, giving speeches, and he missed that interaction. Now he lived a solitary life. He had no family or friends. Only his brother came to visit him from time to time. Sometimes he felt so lonely, he was ready to give up. But he always calmed down afterwards. He knew he could never go back.

As he struggled with the fish, the two joggers approached. Only when the two men were about ten yards away did the old man notice them. He had been so focused on the fish.

The old man watched them approach. He couldn't see their faces because they were hooded. One of the men was tall and slender and the other shorter and stockier. There was something familiar about them.

"How's the fishing?" the tall man said loudly. "Are they hitting today?"

The old man didn't answer. He knew that voice. The men reached him and stopped. The tall man stood in front of him and pushed down his hood, so the old man could see his face. The old man's eyes widened with recognition.

"You!" he said. He let go of his fishing pole. The tall man nodded, saying nothing.

"It's been a long time," the old man said. "I didn't think I would ever see you again."

The tall man nodded silently again.

"What brings you here?"

"Unfinished business," the tall man said.

"I see." The old man reached toward his cooler. "Want a beer?" The tall man shook his head no.

"What about your friend?"

"He doesn't want one either."

"You mind if I have one?"

"Go right ahead."

The old man bent down and opened his cooler. He reached inside, his back toward the two men.

The tall man reached behind his back and pulled out a gun with a silencer from his waistband. He shot the old man once in the head. Blood and brain matter splattered onto the cooler and tackle box. The force of the bullet made the old man stagger forward, so when he crashed to the ground his head splashed in the water.

"*Cabrón!*" The tall man spat on the dead old man. "Dead at last." He turned toward the other man and said, "He was always a tricky one. Check the cooler."

The shorter man put his hand into the cooler and brought it out again with a black short-nosed .38 revolver. He slipped it in the waistband of his jogging suit.

"Aren't you going to shoot him too?" the tall man asked him.

"You're damn right I am," the shorter man said in a gruff voice. "I've waited a long time for this moment."

"Do it then," the tall man said. "We have to go."

The shorter man pulled a large revolver from the back of his jogging suit, much the same way the tall man had done before. He pointed it at the old man.

"No silencer?" the tall man asked him.

"No," the other man said. "I want to hear the sound of the bullet when it hits him."

He fired the gun into the old man's head. The report was very loud and echoed in the empty beach. The force of the bullet took a chunk of the old man's head and made his body twitch in the water.

"Good grief!" the tall man said. "Sounded like a cannon. What kind of a gun is that?"

"A .357 Magnum." The shorter man grinned. "Nice, no?"

"Noisy, for sure." He looked around to see if anyone had seen them, but the beach was deserted still, although the sky was pink already. He put his hood back up. "Let's go."

The two men started jogging rapidly, skirting the coastline, in the same direction they had come. Eventually, they disappeared over the horizon. The sun was rising by then. The beach was still deserted.

The rising tide lapped at the body of the old man, swaying it gently, as if trying to put the old man to sleep. Less than an arm's length away, a glob of the old man's blood and brains glistened in the sun atop the black tackle box, displaying, in a symbolic and sinister parody, the colors of the Cuban Revolution.

*